MW01148110

Rest in Pieces

A Southern Quilting Mystery, Volume 9

Elizabeth Craig

Published by Elizabeth Craig, 2018.

This is a work of fiction. Similarities to real people, places, or events are entirely coincidental.

REST IN PIECES

First edition. April 23, 2018.

Copyright © 2018 Elizabeth Craig.

ISBN: 978-1946227263

Written by Elizabeth Craig.

For Mama and Daddy

Chapter One

Beatrice peered out through one of the windows on the doors leading into the sanctuary. She turned to smile at her daughter, Piper, resplendent in her wedding dress and glowing with happiness. "It's a full house," said Beatrice. "I think most of the town is here."

Piper grinned back at her. "Considering that I'm a local teacher, the mother of the bride is the minister's wife, and the groom's family has lived here forever, that's hardly surprising, is it?"

Piper smoothed down her dress, which didn't really need any smoothing. It was a simple and elegant white satin dress with a drape of tulle from her waist to the floor. She wore a fingertip-length veil over her dark hair. She smiled at Beatrice, who was wearing a waterfall-style jacket with lace applique over a long tank with lace detail and a full-length skirt, all in a silvery gray. "You look beautiful, Mama."

"I was about to say the same to you!" Beatrice blinked rapidly to disperse the pesky tears that kept stinging her eyes. "I wish your father were alive to see this. And to walk you down the aisle. He would have been so proud of the woman you've become."

Piper gave Beatrice a quick hug. "I miss him, too, Mama. But don't worry that I'm somehow missing out on anything. I love having you walk me down the aisle."

"And I love walking you down. But I wanted to give you something to help you feel as though your dad were here, too." Beatrice stooped to pick up a small box. She opened it to reveal a simple gold bracelet with a ring attached. Piper gave a little gasp and slipped it on her wrist. "I know your father would love that you have his old ring."

Piper gave her mother a wordless, grateful look and then hugged her.

Beatrice gave her hand a squeeze as she let her go. She cleared her throat. "The church has never looked lovelier." Beatrice peeked out the window again, taking in the pew ends draped with tulle and baby's breath bouquets. She saw Ash, handsome and relaxed and beaming in a tuxedo, walk out at the front of the church with his father, Ramsay, who looked somewhat less-comfortable in his tuxedo, but still so happy. Beatrice's friend, Meadow, as the mother-of-the-groom, was already seated and kept irrepressibly turning around to look at the back of the sanctuary. She glimpsed Beatrice this time and grinned at her.

Piper's attendants for the ceremony were some of her former students. They were giggling quietly in a group a few feet away from Beatrice and Piper. The church's choir director gestured to them to fall in line, whispering reminders to them and opened the door.

Pachelbel's Canon in D began playing in the sanctuary and Beatrice took a deep, steadying breath. "That's our cue, sweetheart."

But Piper was already at the door, holding her arm out to her.

The church was completely filled with old friends and new. Wyatt smiled at them as they slowly made their way down the aisle to the front of the beautiful, old church. It was a late-afternoon wedding and sunlight streamed through the colorful stained glass onto the wooden pews and the stone walls and floors. A quick glance at her daughter told Beatrice that Piper only had eyes for Ash ... and he for her. Ramsay tugged at his tux and winked at Beatrice as they approached. Then, after a few words, Beatrice sat down in the front pew, watching as her daughter joined her life with Beatrice's new son.

A young soloist friend of Piper's sang *Ave Maria* and Beatrice's eyes prickled again with happy tears at the old hymn. Rings were tenderly exchanged, vows given, and before Beatrice knew it, Piper and Ash were married and striding, glowing, back down the aisle as an usher offered Beatrice his arm to lead her out of the church. Walking down the aisle, she saw her friend, Savannah, give her an approving nod. Her tenderhearted sister, Georgia, was dabbing up her own tears and smiled at her mistily through them. They sat with Posy, who looked to be trying to restrain the unpredictable Miss Sissy from getting up and following Beatrice out of the church.

Beatrice knew that Ash and Piper would be staying back at the church for photos, some even with Wyatt. She and Piper had had photos taken before the ceremony, so she needed to hurry on to the reception site to make sure, once again, that everything was set up and ready to go.

As she drove to the park that sat on the lakefront, Beatrice once again thanked God for the good weather. Piper and Ash had wanted an outdoor reception. Beatrice had realized that this was going to either be absolutely perfect and beautiful or a complete disaster. The weather was ideal and the location was, too: with the Blue Ridge mountains rising before them and the sun glinting on the small lake. They had tents set up and Beatrice's quick walk-through, her second of the day, showed that everything was in order.

Piper had taken inspiration from past weddings and incorporated quilting into the decorating of the tents. Hanging quilts added texture to the white tents and blocks adding a pop of color to the white tablecloths of all the tables. Ash's favorite cuisine was his mother's food, and to prevent a determined Meadow from leaving her mother-of-the-groom duties to cook, they'd hired a caterer who had Southern cooking nailed. The aroma of fried chicken wafted on the gentle breeze. The crowning glory was June Bug's marvelous wedding cake. It was, naturally, in a quilted design, a diamond hexagonal quilting with fresh flowers adorning the top. Beatrice's mouth started watering. She knew from experience how delectable June Bug's cakes were and she remembered that Piper had bucked tradition and opted for a chocolate cake with raspberry filling and buttercream icing.

Beatrice was still admiring the cake when she spotted June Bug standing shyly at the edge of the tent. "June Bug, this looks like an absolute masterpiece. And I know from past experience that your wedding cakes taste just as good as they look, which is amazing because I remember eating wedding cakes back in Atlanta, and they all tasted like cardboard."

June Bug smiled at her, eyes twinkling. "I made it *especially* good today, since it's for Piper."

"Did you make it to the ceremony?" asked Beatrice, frowning a bit. "I should remember, but all I saw was a blur of people."

"I made it there. And it was lovely," said June Bug. "Then I ran over here as fast as I could. I sat in the balcony."

Then there was no time left to talk as the guests started arriving at the reception. Beatrice had put June Bug's eight-year-old niece, Katy, in charge of the guestbook. Her serious expression changed to smiles when she saw Beatrice. Katy's straight brown hair was pulled back with a blue ribbon that matched her carefully-starched blue dress. She gave Beatrice a shy wave and Beatrice gave her a quick hug. "Thanks for taking this on again, Katy. You did such a great job with the guestbook last time."

Katy flushed at the compliment and said in her quiet voice, "Thanks for asking me."

As guests walked in, the catering staff lit candles on each of the tables, lending a warm glow to the insides of the tents. Guests filed up to Beatrice to tell her how beautiful the wedding had been. The band was finishing setting up their equipment and was quietly warming up. Savannah, Georgia, and Posy came up and hugged Beatrice.

"I've finally stopped crying," said Georgia with a light laugh. "I don't know why I got so emotional. It was just such a lovely wedding." She gave Beatrice a quick hug.

Savannah said in an approving tone, "And very organized. The ushers behaved perfectly. They were practically in military precision."

A smile touched Beatrice's lips. Savannah always admired symmetry of any kind. Her quilts usually reflected this.

Posy said, "I especially loved seeing all the young people in the ceremony. I'm guessing those precious children were Piper's former students?"

Beatrice nodded her head. "They were girls that have kept up with Piper through the last couple of years. Sometimes they'll pop by the school to see her and show Piper how much they've grown and what they're up to. Piper loves it."

Georgia said, "They looked so proud to be part of the big day. And they all wore white, too!"

Beatrice said with a smile, "Piper thought it would be easier if they simply wore whatever white dress they had instead of making them all buy the same dress. That way, most of them wore their Easter dresses or could have easily borrowed a dress from a friend."

"It was good the children could be Piper's attendants, since you needed to walk her down the aisle," said Savannah in her brusque, practical way.

Beatrice said, "Very true." She glanced around. "Where's Miss Sissy?"

"Near the food, of course," said Posy with a laugh.

Sure enough, Beatrice spotted Miss Sissy with a plate heaped with fried chicken, ham biscuits, and green beans. She appeared deep in concentration as she tried to find room on her plate for fried green tomatoes.

Savannah also spotted Miss Sissy's plate and quickly said, "Lovely wedding, Beatrice," and started hurrying over to the food as if there might not be much left after Miss Sissy descended on it.

Georgia said ruefully, "I guess she's getting hungry."

Posy said, "Who isn't? I've been to a couple of weddings this caterer has done. Her macaroni and cheese is to die for."

Beatrice nodded. "Her mashed potatoes, too. I went to the tasting with Piper."

Posy added, "And her biscuits were so light and fluffy."

Now everyone was looking over at the food tent.

A car pulled up with a jaunty toot of its horn and Beatrice said, "Oh, they're here!" Piper and Ash jumped out of the car and were instantly surrounded by guests. Wyatt pulled up in his own car a moment later and was also soon engulfed.

Georgia said, "You really should have something to eat, Beatrice. It's been a big day for you, and it's not ending anytime soon."

Beatrice said ruefully, "Yes, but if I brave the food tables, I'll be swarmed by guests and won't be able to eat it."

Posy said quickly, "I'll bring you a plate, Beatrice. Everyone will be distracted by the bride and groom ... and Meadow, too! That will give you a chance to eat. I'll make it a big plate and maybe Wyatt can have a few bites, too."

Beatrice thanked her and watched as Posy quickly made her way to the tables, ducking in and dodging conversation with a gentle smile as she focused on her task. Beatrice was so deep in thought that she jumped a little as Wyatt slipped an arm around her. Beatrice grinned up at him.

"Happy?" he asked.

"Very. Even better now that you're here. How did the pictures go? It didn't seem as though they took very long."

Wyatt said, "That was the best part. The photographer really knew what he was doing, apparently. He got exactly what he wanted and then let us leave." He paused. "It looks as though everyone is having a good time."

"Everyone is having a *wonderful* time!" bellowed an enthusiastic voice behind them. Beatrice and Wyatt didn't have the chance to turn around before Meadow grabbed them both into a bear hug. Her gray hair was still in its long braid, although it was somewhat more tamed than usual, with fewer strands falling out. But otherwise, she looked wildly different from her usual self. Ordinarily, Meadow was a fan of mismatched, flowing clothes in bright colors. Today she wore a beige coat dress, carefully-applied makeup, and tottered on an unfamiliar pair of heels. She suddenly lurched as she tried to turn and face them, causing Wyatt to grip her arm to keep her steady.

"Isn't this the happiest day ever?" she asked, beaming. She gave Beatrice another hug, weaving alarmingly again on her heels. "Piper looks so beautiful. And Ash so handsome!" Her eyes filled up with tears and as she tried blinking them away, they tumbled out on her flushed cheeks, causing her to rummage through her purse for a tissue.

After giving a robustly blowing her nose, she added, "And everyone came! Honestly, they *did*, didn't they? I swear that the entire town is here." She frowned. "In fact, I'm pretty sure that there are people here that we didn't invite. Piper's list and yours were fairly short and I know exactly who was on Ash's, Ramsay's, and my list."

Posy slipped Beatrice a heaping plate, napkins, and forks and Beatrice gave her a grateful smile. Then she turned back to Meadow. "*Who* isn't supposed to be here?"

"Well, for instance, Ophelia Lundy over there." Meadow wrinkled her nose.

Beatrice followed her gaze and saw a small, child-like woman with a sharp-featured face and a short shock of blunt-cut white hair. She had a cagey, observant expression as she watched the guests. It was difficult to gauge her age ... she might have been seventy-five, but she might have been sixty. Beatrice watched her, thoughtfully, while she gobbled down some of the fried chicken.

"She wasn't on *my* list," said Beatrice. "I don't even recognize her. She's from Dappled Hills?"

Wyatt said, looking alarmed, "You don't recognize her? She's a member of my congregation. I should have introduced you to her."

Beatrice frowned. "Has she been *coming* to church? She's fairly distinctive-looking. Surely I'd have remembered if she'd been regularly attending."

Meadow shook her head. "I haven't seen her there in a while. Which is fine with me." She crossed her arms and pursed her lips, disapprovingly. "Ophelia gets into everyone's business. She's very nosy! You can look at her right now and see that she's trying to gather intel."

"Intel?" asked Wyatt, a grin pulling at his lips. "I didn't realize that she was a spy. I've always thought of her as a rather innocuous member of my congregation."

Meadow said, "That's because you're too trusting! No, I promise you, she's out looking for dirt on everyone. That's her main hobby. That and casting blame on other people as if she's perfect."

"Which I take it, she's not?" asked Beatrice, eyebrows raised. She took a bite of the creamy mac and cheese and then offered the plate to Wyatt. "Try the pasta," she said.

Meadow snorted. "Clearly. Although you wouldn't know it to hear her talk. She acts as if smoking is a terrible sin, but then her teeth are quite yellow and her clothes smell like smoke. She acts holier-than-thou about drinking, but *she* drinks. I've seen her buying alcohol at the grocery store ... and not just a little here and there. Bottles! And bottles!"

Wyatt said mildly, "Maybe she's pointing out faults in others that she wishes she didn't have, herself."

"Maybe she should just keep her ideas about others' faults to herself," said Meadow. She sighed. "Well, I suppose we'll just ignore the fact that she's crashed the wedding. There's no point in creating a scene by asking her to leave. I need to run and meet and greet everyone anyway. And get food! That plate of food that Posy made you is making my stomach growl." She hurried off, still tottering dangerously on her heels, and was soon surrounded by guests.

The band played a romantic slow number and Piper and Ash started dancing. Wyatt and Beatrice quickly finished up eating. "That food is too good to hurry through, but we're short on time. We're up next," he said with a smile.

"Good thing I have my dancing shoes on," said Beatrice. She held out a foot encased in gray heels ... carefully chosen low heels that she could actually dance in.

"Do you think Meadow will be able to manage a dance?" asked Wyatt with a chuckle.

"I guess we'll find out!"

Meadow was able to stay on her feet for a dance with Ramsay, although Ramsay's eyes were wide and he had a panicked expression on his face whenever she lurched at him. Beatrice relaxed in Wyatt's arms as they moved on a dance floor under strings of fairy lights. As the sun went down, the tents looked even more magical with their glow.

After the first song, Ramsay danced with Beatrice, and Wyatt and Meadow danced together. Ramsay said dryly, "It's nice to dance with someone without fear that they'll collapse on the floor or stab me in the foot with a heel."

Beatrice laughed. "Fortunately, it's a slower song, so Wyatt won't have to worry as much about keeping Meadow upright."

"She was determined to wear those heels," he said with a shake of his head. "And you know how stubborn she can be." He gave her a small twirl and then said, "There's something I've been meaning to ask you."

Beatrice laughed. "What I'm reading now?"

"Am I really that transparent?" asked Ramsay in mock consternation. "Surely I could have asked you about something else. Your opinion on local politics? Favorite foods?"

"That wouldn't have been in keeping with our usual conversations, Ramsay. Although I can't think why I seem to be the only person you talk about books with. There are plenty of readers in Dappled Hills," said Beatrice. "Your wife is one of them. In fact, it was Meadow who recommended my current book to me."

"Meadow? Sadly, she doesn't share my taste in literature," said Ramsay, pulling a face. "Her interests run more along the lines of thrillers."

"I'm not altogether certain that *we* share the same tastes in literature. I seem to remember your giving me *Moby Dick* to read right before my wedding," said Beatrice.

Ramsay said, "That was just bad timing! And I'm counting on you to try it again when life settles down a little."

"To answer your question, I'm reading *A Tree Grows in Brooklyn*. But it's taking me forever to read because I've been so busy with Piper's wedding. How about you?" asked Beatrice.

Ramsay grinned at her, "You won't believe it if I tell you."

Beatrice raised her eyebrows. "You're not *finally* giving *Pride and Prejudice* a go, are you? I've been recommending that book to you forever!"

"Well now, you know I've been busy. Catching bad guys, and all that."

Beatrice said, "What do you think of it?"

"I love it," admitted Ramsay. "And somehow I thought it was going to be awful because it was all about wanting weddings and marriages, and that's all that's been going on in my house for the last few months. But it's a fantastic book. I'm going to reread it as soon as I finish."

They danced for a moment in silence and then Ramsay glanced around them at the lights, the decorations, and the food. "You and Piper really pulled together a beautiful wedding."

"Oh, well, we had help. Meadow had lots of good ideas. But in the end, it was mostly Piper, you know. I was busy trying to adjust to married life, combine two households, and get used to a new role in the church," said Beatrice.

"It sure is packed," said Ramsay. He gave a small frown. "I'm surprised you invited Ophelia Lundy. She's one of the town residents who causes a bit more trouble than some of the others. How do you know her?"

"Meadow was asking me the same thing. I *don't* know her. She's apparently a wedding crasher," said Beatrice with a shrug.

"Great," said Ramsay with a sigh. "Well, no worries. I'll keep an eye on her."

"Is she that bad?" asked Beatrice.

"Sometimes. She can just get into arguments with folks at the drop of a hat. Somehow Ophelia knows *everything* that goes on in town and I think she's one of those people who likes to be in the know. It'll be okay—don't worry," said Ramsay hastily, obviously not wanting to create any sort of blemish on the day.

The dance ended and then there were toasts for the couple, with Beatrice giving the first one. She was determined to keep the tone light, never being fond of public tears for herself or anyone else. Still, she couldn't help but get a little choked up and quickly ended her toast with a hug for Piper and Ash. Ash followed with a toast, and then Ramsay. Soon there were toasts from other friends and guests, including Barton Perry, who was running for state senate and was an elder at Wyatt's church.

After the toasts, the dancing recommenced with livelier tunes that the younger people were dancing to. Beatrice took a seat at one of the tables but was immediately swarmed by guests wanting to speak to the mother of the bride. She ended up standing again in a sort of impromptu receiving line when Meadow joined her. Quite some time later, she plopped down again, exhausted, Meadow dropping into a chair beside her.

Meadow instantly kicked off her shoes and gave a melodramatic groan. "I'm going to sleep well tonight, I think. But it's been the perfect day. The wedding ceremony was a tear-jerker, the food is fabulous, the cake will be sure to melt in everyone's mouth, and the band hasn't missed a beat. It's the best wedding ever."

"Isn't it wonderful that all our friends could be here to share today with us?" asked Meadow happily, her gaze scanning the crowd. A small crease furrowed her brow. "Except that I have the funny feeling I've forgotten something. I think I was supposed to remember something. From a few days ago."

Beatrice said dryly, "A few days ago feels like decades. We've done a lot to help Piper and Ash with the final details of the reception."

"That's true. But I know that Posy wanted to talk with me about something. She was worried about … somebody." Meadow shrugged and sighed. "It's gone. Poof! Anyway, I'll probably run by the quilt shop and check in with her tomorrow after it opens. Want to go?"

"Maybe. But I might just stay at home in my pajamas all day, too," said Beatrice. "This has been quite a week."

"But don't you agree? It's the best wedding ever?" asked Meadow.

Beatrice grinned at her. "The very best. And I think I've spoken to every guest, at least once."

"Except for Ophelia," said Meadow, making a face. "She didn't want to come up and say hi for obvious reasons. And now it looks as if she's stirring the pot." She waved her hand to indicate someone a couple of tables away.

Chapter Two

Ophelia was grinning in an unpleasant way at Pearl Perry, wife of the state senate candidate. Pearl, as usual, was perfectly attired in a crisp and rather matronly dress without a hair out of place. The only difference in her usual appearance was the stress that was evident on Pearl's delicate features.

"Perhaps Pearl is wondering how best to escape from Ophelia's company," mused Beatrice to Meadow.

They watched as Pearl opened up her purse, pulled something out, and leaned toward Ophelia in a quietly conspiratorial way, reaching her hand and its contents out to Ophelia and peering earnestly at her.

Ophelia's face contorted with fury and she slapped Pearl's hand away, causing money to fly at Pearl, falling in her lap, the table, and the ground beneath.

"How *dare* you!" snarled Ophelia. "I'll have you know that I have *plenty* of money! Gobs of it!" She stood up, kicking the chair out of the way, and stormed out of the reception.

"Lovely," said Beatrice dryly. "All we needed was a huge scene at the wedding to draw attention away from Piper and

Ash's big day. Thanks, Ophelia. And I hope Pearl is all right. She looks as if she wants to disappear into the floor."

Meadow said, "How absolutely ridiculous! Maybe *everyone* didn't see that, although the way that they're looking sure makes me think that they did. It'll be the talk of the town tomorrow, even though I think only the closest tables *heard* it. Thank heaven for the loud band in the background."

"Here comes Pearl now," said Beatrice. "Judging from the expression on her face, it looks like she knows we spotted her altercation with Ophelia."

Pearl's normally-pale features were infused with a blotchy flush. She held her arms crossed across her body in a defensive posture.

"I'm so, so sorry about that," she said quickly to Beatrice and Meadow. "What a terrible thing to create a scene on such a beautiful and special occasion." She glanced quickly around her as if to gauge how many of the wedding guests might have witnessed her argument with Ophelia. Pearl's husband, Barton, was in a conversation with a small group of people but Beatrice saw him watching them through narrowed eyes.

Meadow said firmly in the tone of someone who wishes something to be true, "I don't think that anyone really noticed—just a small handful of people. Is everything all right?"

Pearl blinked. "Yes. Well, at least, I suppose so. I was surprised to see Ophelia here."

"So were we," said Meadow ruefully. "Neither Beatrice nor I invited her."

"When I saw her here a few minutes ago, I remembered hearing that she'd come upon some hard times recently," said

Pearl in a rush. "And I think she has a local relative who isn't good about helping Ophelia out. I tried to discreetly give Ophelia a little money, just to tide her over a bit. And, well, you saw what happened." The blotchy redness was now creeping down Pearl's neck. "She totally lost it."

"That was very kind of you," said Meadow, beaming at Pearl.

"Was it? I don't know. With Barton running for office and everything, I suppose it's simply reminded me of my civic duties. I was only trying to help." But Pearl looked away as she said the words and Beatrice had the feeling that she knew more than she was saying. Then Pearl quickly changed tack. She glanced back at Beatrice with somewhat misty eyes. "It's been such a lovely wedding," she said. "They look so happy together."

Beatrice, never a fan of tears, said quickly, "There's something about weddings that really brings out the emotion in us, isn't there?"

Pearl said, "Something." She brushed her eyes impatiently with her hand and said earnestly to Beatrice and Meadow, "I hope they're as happy in 25 years as they are tonight." She steadied herself. "By the way, Beatrice, I feel terrible about this, but Barton and I forgot to bring Piper's and Ash's wedding gift here. I should have mailed it to them sooner, anyway. I'm so sorry. I'm guessing they're going directly out of town for their honeymoon? I'll bring it over to your house tomorrow morning."

"Oh, don't worry about that. In fact, I have some errands tomorrow morning and would be happy to drop by and pick it up," said Beatrice. There went any plans of staying in pajamas. But Beatrice didn't really mind because she knew that sometimes when she was truly exhausted, that's when she ended up with the most frenetic energy.

"Are you sure? That would be great," said Pearl.

Beatrice was about to respond to her when Meadow gasped. "They're about to cut the cake!" She grabbed Beatrice's arm and they hurried over, the crowd of guests around the cake table parting for the mothers of the bride and groom and making room for them at the very front.

June Bug's magnificent cake was another crowning achievement, as Beatrice had known it would be. It was gorgeous to look at and moist and delicious to eat. She somehow managed to have enough time to actually savor a slice before needing to talk with anyone else. And she and Wyatt were able to slip in several more dances before Piper threw her bouquet and the happy couple left for their honeymoon under a full moon and a sky dotted with stars.

The next morning, Beatrice woke up with a smile on her face. It had been such a wonderful evening that it almost felt like a dream. She tried to move quietly, so as not to wake Wyatt. It was Sunday morning, and usually that meant they were both at the church. But they'd planned ahead to take this day off, and a new associate minister at the church was at the helm this morning. Sometimes Wyatt was able to sleep in if Beatrice were quiet enough when she got out of bed. She turned to look at him and was surprised to see that he wasn't there.

Beatrice pulled on a robe and slippers and walked into the living room to see Wyatt slipping back in the house with a smiling Noo-noo on a leash. He spotted Beatrice and smiled, holding up a paper bag.

"I decided to walk downtown with Noo-noo and get some muffins from June Bug's shop," said Wyatt, stooping to take the leash off the little corgi.

Beatrice said, "You sure were quiet! I thought you were still in the bed. Or maybe I was sleeping so soundly that I didn't hear a thing."

"I think all the excitement of the night before kept me awake. I finally decided to stop tossing and turning and get up. June Bug's shop opens early and after that delicious cake last night, I was in the mood for more of her baking," said Wyatt, leaning over to give Beatrice a light kiss. He washed his hands in the kitchen and pulled out two plates.

Beatrice poured them both coffee and then settled down at the kitchen table. "I must have been more worn out than I thought to have slept that hard. It was a beautiful wedding, although I haven't spoken to so many people at an event since I was a museum curator."

"Everyone looked like they were having fun," said Wyatt. He pulled out blueberry and banana nut muffins and put them on the plates, then frowned for a second. "Was everything all right between Pearl and Ophelia? At one point when I was speaking to someone, I glanced over and it looked as though they were having a disagreement of some kind." Noo-noo, still panting a little from her walk, tried to inconspicuously get directly under Wyatt so that she could see any muffin crumbs that might fall. She wanted to ensure that the crumbs never reached the floor.

"They were, although I'm not sure it was for the reason that Pearl was saying. She indicated that she'd heard Ophelia had fallen on hard times and she was trying to lend her money, surreptitiously. But Ophelia seemed quite offended and yelled that she had plenty of money. Pearl ended up dropping the money all over the floor and Ophelia stormed away. It was all very dramatic." Beatrice buttered the muffins, which were still warm and gave a happy sigh After a few moments she asked, "Do you think that Ophelia is doing as well as she says? Should the church do anything to help?"

Wyatt shook his head slowly. "She certainly doesn't live very high on the hog, but I've never had any indication from her that she was having any sort of financial difficulty. And the church can help, but only if we're asked. It sounds as though Ophelia might be too proud to ask for help, if she needs it at all. I've always had the impression that she just leads a very simple life."

Beatrice snapped her fingers and glanced over at the clock on the kitchen wall. "Going back to Pearl, I did tell her that I was going to be running errands this morning and would stop by her house to pick up a wedding present for Piper and Ash. I should finish eating this and then head on out. I'm getting something of a late start today."

"I could go with you, if you don't mind combining errands. I'm not going to the church until later today, and I do have a couple of things I need to take care of," said Wyatt.

After Beatrice got ready, they headed out with Beatrice behind the wheel. They drove to the grocery store and the drugstore before driving to Barton and Pearl's house. It was one of the larger homes in Dappled Hills, a brick Colonial with mountain views. It was directly next to the lakefront park where Piper and Ash had their wedding reception.

Beatrice parked in the driveway. "I'll just ring the doorbell and pop right back to the car," she said. "Won't be but a minute."

She'd hopped out of the car and was walking to the front door when Barton Perry came staggering around the side of the house. His still-handsome face was white with shock as he wordlessly held out his hands to Beatrice. Instead of his usual suit and bowtie, he was wearing track pants and a gray tee shirt.

"Barton? What's wrong?" asked Beatrice sharply.

"Dead," said Barton, eyes open wide.

"*Who's* dead?" asked Beatrice, hurrying to his side. Wyatt got out of the car and walked toward them, his face concerned.

"Pearl." The name came out in a kind of groan.

"In the backyard?" asked Beatrice.

"I'll call Red," said Wyatt, pulling his phone out of his pocket. He followed closely behind Beatrice as she walked around the side of the house. Barton leaned against the hood of Beatrice's car, head in his hands.

In Pearl's lovely backyard, full of brightly-flowering shrubs and plants, was Pearl. She was slumped on her side, a large, broken flowerpot lying next to her head.

Chapter Three

"Ramsay is on his way," Wyatt said grimly.

Beatrice, who'd checked unsuccessfully for Pearl's pulse, gave a sigh. "Who on earth could have done such a thing?" asked Beatrice. "Pearl was just out gardening." She looked more closely at Pearl this time. She was wearing gardening gloves and a hat, and a pile of weeds lay next to her. It almost looked as though she'd decided to take an inopportune nap in the middle of her gardening.

Wyatt shook his head. "I don't know." He sighed. "I'm going to make sure Barton is all right."

Beatrice heard a car pulling quickly up to the house. "That's probably Ramsay. I'll never get used to how quick the response time is here. I'll go with you."

Barton was still slumped against Beatrice's car, his head in his hands. Ramsay jumped out of his police cruiser and looked at Beatrice and Wyatt. "Where is she?" he asked.

They pointed to the backyard and Ramsay, getting on his phone, hurried back there.

Barton raised his head and gave them a weary look. "I can't believe this."

Beatrice said gently, "We're so sorry, Barton. What a terrible thing to have to go through."

Barton held out his hands and seemed to be searching for words. "It was just a normal morning. Pearl wanted to do some weeding before it got too warm outside. I went to the gym. When I came home, I thought Pearl would be in the house by then since there wasn't that much work to do in the yard. I couldn't find her, so I walked into the backyard and saw...." Barton stopped talking and gestured vaguely with his hands toward the back of the house. "I have no idea who might have done this to Pearl. She did nothing to deserve this. She was a good woman and everyone respected her."

Beatrice nodded. "That's definitely true." She paused. "Did she have anything on her mind lately? At the wedding last night, she seemed sort of ... well, she got a little teared up."

"Weddings had that effect on her," said Barton, looking away. "But no, she didn't say that she had anything on her mind. Not last night and not today, either. All she wanted to do was to come out and work in the yard for a while."

Wyatt said, "Sometimes yardwork can be cathartic. That's one of the best ways for me to work off any stress that I have."

"And my yard is so happy that you've moved in to tame it," said Beatrice with a small smile. She took a deep breath and then said, "Barton, do you have any idea why Ophelia would have had words with Pearl at the wedding last night?"

Barton frowned, brow crinkling. "I didn't know anything about that. But then, I did get caught up in a long conversation with someone, so maybe I missed it. I did see the two of you speaking, of course. Since you were the mother of the bride, that was very normal. Although I noticed at the time that Pearl seemed a little emotional. I figured it was probably because of the wedding and just some rising emotions."

Beatrice said, "I think Pearl was embarrassed about the scene between her and Ophelia. Pearl said that she tried to offer Ophelia money because she thought she wasn't doing well, financially. But Ophelia became really enraged and practically threw the money back at her, insisting that she didn't have any money problems."

Barton shook his head slowly. "It sounds like Pearl, since she certainly always had other people on her mind. But she didn't mention anything to me about it. We were tired when we came home last night and didn't talk about the wedding or really about anything else. Maybe she would have mentioned it to me today." Deep lines of grief showed in his haggard face.

Ramsay strode back around the house toward them. "The state police are on their way." He shook his head. "I'm so sorry about this, Barton. Do you want to head inside the house and have a seat? Maybe get something to drink? I'm going to chat with Wyatt and Beatrice for a few minutes and then I'll come in and ask you a few questions. I promise we'll get to the bottom of this."

Barton pushed away from the car and said quietly, "Actually, I would like to go inside for a while. Thanks, Ramsay."

They watched him go inside and then Ramsay said glumly, "What a mess. And now I'm saddled with a high-profile murder, at that, considering Barton is getting geared up for a run at the state senate office. What did you two see when you came here?"

"Not very much," admitted Wyatt.

Beatrice said, "When we arrived, it seemed as though Barton had just discovered Pearl's body. He came around the side of the house, looking really shaken."

"Out of curiosity, what *were* you two doing over here?" asked Ramsay. "This isn't really a place you come over to hang out at, is it?"

"Not usually, no. Pearl had a wedding present for Piper and Ash and I told her I'd swing by this morning and pick it up," said Beatrice. "I guess we'll get it to them eventually—there's certainly no hurry."

Ramsay said, "I'd imagine that the state police will want to go through the house and make sure there's nothing that gives a clue to Pearl's death. I let Barton go back in since his fingerprints are all over the house anyway, and since there's no sign of a break-in and poor Pearl was found outside." He stared at the house for a moment, as if collecting his thoughts. "Did Barton tell either of you where he was when Pearl was murdered?"

Wyatt answered, "He said that he'd been to the gym this morning and found Pearl when he came back home."

Ramsay said, "Well, that would explain his clothing. I think this might have been the first time I've ever seen Barton without a suit and a bowtie. They're practically his uniform."

Beatrice said, "Did Meadow tell you about the argument that Ophelia and Pearl had last night? Well, I guess it wasn't really an *argument* because it was one-sided. Ophelia was angry at Pearl and not the other way around."

Ramsay snapped his fingers. "I knew there was something I wanted to ask you two. Yes, of course Meadow told me about it—you know how she is. She said that Pearl told you two that it was about Ophelia's finances? Some such thing?"

"Pearl said she was trying to help and that Ophelia didn't want help," said Beatrice.

"I wish Ophelia wouldn't want help on a more regular basis," said Ramsay, dryly. "She calls me up a couple or more times a week to have me help her with all sorts of minor things. That's what she seems to think the local police is all about. Sometimes she's complaining about a neighbor, sometimes she's reporting people littering in town, sometimes she wants help moving furniture or reaching something on a top shelf. Ophelia can be a real handful."

Beatrice asked, "Do you think Ophelia is unstable in any way? Could she have come over here and continued her argument with Pearl? Maybe even have let the argument get out of hand and then smashed her over the head with the flowerpot?"

Ramsay tilted his head to one side. "I just don't know. Yes, she can be ornery. Yes, she has a temper. Do I see her bashing people over the head with flowerpots? I'm not sure. She's not a particularly young woman and that was a rather heavy flowerpot. But do you know what you could do to help me out? You and Wyatt could run by and check in on her for a couple of minutes for me. Right now, she's the only suspect I know of and I'd like to make sure she's sticking around the house until I wrap up here and have a chance to talk to her. Think you could trump up some reason to keep her occupied for a while?"

Wyatt said, "I was just telling Beatrice that I should run by to visit Ophelia. I haven't seen her in church lately. And Beatrice didn't even know who she was before the wedding, so I could take the opportunity to introduce her to another member of the congregation."

"That would be perfect. Tell her how wonderful it was to see her at the wedding—even if it wasn't," said Ramsay. "And, while you're out, do you mind dropping by and doing a wellness visit on Miss Sissy, too? Meadow has been trying to call her cell phone and it's been going straight to voice mail."

"Miss Sissy has voice mail?" asked Beatrice.

Ramsay snorted. "Ash helped her set it up before the wedding. You should dial it. It features Miss Sissy snapping 'who's there?' and then a beep."

"Sounds likely," said Wyatt with a chuckle.

Ramsay said, "I'll stay here and talk to Barton, get his statement, and then talk to the state police when they come. If you could maybe keep an eye on Ophelia for an hour? Just keep her there at the house so that I can have a chance to ask her a few questions. Once I fill in the state police and make sure the scene is secure, I can zip over there and y'all can zip back out again."

"Will do," said Beatrice. They climbed into the car and Beatrice started the engine. "So to Miss Sissy's, first, I'm assuming? That would be the quicker visit, since we're supposed to be keeping Ophelia occupied for an hour. Thank goodness we didn't get any refrigerated items at the grocery store or else they'd all be spoiled by now. Where does Ophelia live, anyway?"

"It's sort of off the beaten path. Once we're finished at Miss Sissy's, I'll direct you there." Wyatt was quiet for a minute and then said, "I just can't believe this. Poor Pearl. And murdered in her own backyard while she was working with her flowers."

"I know. What puzzles me is why no one saw anything. Wouldn't there have been a car parked outside Pearl's house? Wouldn't Barton or a neighbor have seen it?" asked Beatrice.

"But, remember, they live right next to the park. There are people coming and going there all day long without anyone really paying attention. Someone could easily have parked there or even on the curb in between Pearl's house and the park and walked over there without being noticed," said Wyatt.

"Yes, but that takes some premeditation," said Beatrice. "And the murder seemed almost as if it were in the heat of the moment. The murderer took advantage of the weapon that was at hand—a heavy flowerpot. It made the crime seem more spontaneous."

"Maybe the killer was planning simply on walking in the park and noticed on the way there that Pearl's car was in the driveway and Barton's wasn't," said Wyatt. "He might have seen that as the perfect opportunity."

Miss Sissy's house was very near their home. It was, like their cottage, a small place. It had always reminded Beatrice of Sleeping Beauty's castle—not because of its size or its occupant, but because of the thorny vines growing threateningly and abundantly around the house, nearly choking out any sign of the brick beneath it.

They walked up to the house and Miss Sissy swung the door open immediately, as if she'd been watching their approach from a dusty window. The old woman gave Wyatt a simpering smile and then glowered at Beatrice as if she were a third wheel for their visit.

Beatrice gritted her teeth into a smile. "Good to see that you're all right, Miss Sissy. Ramsay said that Meadow had been trying to call you and that her calls had gone straight to voicemail. We just wanted to make sure that everything was fine."

Miss Sissy shrugged a thin shoulder. "Lost the phone."

Beatrice blinked at her. This was the cell phone, admittedly not a very expensive one, that she herself had bought for her. "Lost it?"

"Lost it!" snapped Miss Sissy, a bit louder, as if Beatrice were becoming very hard of hearing.

Wyatt said gently, "It's good to see that you're well. We'll come back later and help you look for the phone."

Beatrice was thinking that coming back to search for an errant phone might be an excellent errand for Wyatt to run, solo. She said in an impatient voice, "We'll see you soon, Miss Sissy. Right now, Wyatt and I have to run visit someone."

"Who?" The old woman's eyes squinted suspiciously at Beatrice.

"Ophelia Lundy," said Wyatt.

Miss Sissy squawked. "*I'll* drive you there! Want to give her a piece of my mind about fussing at weddings!"

Beatrice winced at the idea of Miss Sissy driving them anywhere. Miss Sissy was fond of driving on sidewalks and then yelling at the innocent people who were walking on them for being 'road hogs.' "I think it would be better if we saw her ourselves, Miss Sissy. We're not going there to upset her. We want to visit."

Miss Sissy considered this, head tilted so that strands of wiry gray hair tumbled out of the loosely-gathered knot of hair on the top of her head. Then she said firmly, "I'll go. But I'll be good. Wanted to ask her something, anyway. She's a friend of mine."

From everything Beatrice had heard about Ophelia, this seemed likely. The two old women were equally difficult, it seemed. They would have a lot in common.

Wyatt and Beatrice looked at each other. Beatrice sighed and said, "All right, then. Come on. And *I'm* driving. But I don't think it's going to be that exciting of a visit for you. And we have to stay for a while—we wanted to visit for about an hour."

This made Miss Sissy study Beatrice through narrowed eyes. Miss Sissy knew that Beatrice wasn't one to enjoy visiting very much. Then the old woman shrugged and they were on their way.

Beatrice said, "Wyatt, what can you tell me about Ophelia? I need to have something to talk about with her for the space of an hour."

"Doesn't mind her own business!" growled Miss Sissy.

"Yes, I got that," said Beatrice mildly. "Wyatt, do you have anything to add to that? I hardly think I can fill up an hour asking Ophelia about any local gossip that she's picked up."

Wyatt said, "She's actually quite a reader. I frequently see her coming in and out of the library."

Beatrice said in a relieved voice, "Well, that's good. At least I can talk with her about books."

Miss Sissy cackled. "Can't! She reads romance."

"Oh well. Maybe I can find out more about the genre," said Beatrice mildly.

Wyatt gave Beatrice directions until they pulled up in front of Ophelia's house. It was surrounded by tall shrubs and trees that obscured it from the road. The driveway was unpaved and led to the small brick home.

"Won't have to knock," said Miss Sissy. "Never locks her door."

"Still, I think knocking is in order," said Beatrice. "I don't think Wyatt and I want to walk in on Ophelia."

Miss Sissy sighed impatiently.

They walked up a narrow walkway to the house. Wyatt stopped, frowning. "Hold up. The door is open."

Beatrice said, "I suppose I understand not *locking* a door in this town, but leaving it wide open?"

Miss Sissy sniffed. "Probably spying on neighbors."

Beatrice murmured, "Yes, I did hear that Ophelia can be rather nosy." She strode forward and knocked loudly on the open door. "Ophelia? It's Beatrice, Wyatt, and Miss Sissy. May we come in?"

There was no response.

Beatrice and Wyatt gave each other a wary look.

"Maybe we should call her on the phone," said Beatrice. "Do you have her phone number, Wyatt? Or Miss Sissy?"

But Miss Sissy had taken matters into her own hands and had galloped into the little house. "Ophelia!" she bellowed.

Beatrice rolled her eyes at Wyatt and they hurried in behind her. Beatrice's blood ran cold at the sudden, terrified shriek from farther inside the dim home.

Chapter Four

"Miss Sissy?" called Beatrice, rushing toward the shrieking.

Miss Sissy exploded from the back of the house, hands waving, eyes wide. She clutched Wyatt's arm. "Dead! Dead!"

"Ophelia is dead?" asked Wyatt, putting an arm around the old woman.

Miss Sissy nodded her head emphatically.

Beatrice said, "I'll make sure we don't need to call an ambulance." She strode to the back of the house in the direction of Ophelia's bedroom. There she saw Ophelia, dressed for the day, sprawled in the middle of the hall. Next to her was a bottle of wine. Beatrice checked for a pulse.

Wyatt, who had apparently deposited Miss Sissy somewhere outside of the house, came up behind her and sighed. "Anything?" he asked.

Beatrice shook her head. "Could you turn on that hall light?"

Wyatt carefully took his shirt sleeve to avoid erasing any fingerprints the police might search for and turned the light on.

Beatrice stood close to Ophelia's body, studying it.

"Her death definitely wasn't by natural causes," said Beatrice. "Her head is lying in a pool of blood."

Wyatt shook his head sadly. "I'd hoped that maybe it was a natural death and that she never felt a thing. I hate to think that she was afraid at the end of her life."

Beatrice said, "Maybe she wasn't afraid. She likely knew her attacker. Maybe she was simply taken by surprise. It certainly looks as though the wine bottle was the weapon. And her back must have been facing her attacker, so it should have been someone that she trusted. Can you call Ramsay? I can't believe this day."

There was a holler from outside and Wyatt said quickly, "I'll keep an eye on Miss Sissy, too."

As Wyatt pulled his phone out of his pocket and walked toward the front door, Beatrice carefully walked back into the living room and glanced around. She noticed something that she hadn't picked up on the way into the house—the fact that the living room was in great disorder. And not just the disorder of an untidy room. There were drawers pulled out and the contents thrown on the floor as if the killer had been searching for something. The rest of Ophelia's house was rather tidy and it was obvious that she hadn't been the one to make such a mess.

Beatrice stepped cautiously over to the desk in the corner of the room. It was also messy with papers strewn everywhere. She glanced at the papers and then frowned. She saw keys on the floor next to the desk, as if they'd been thrown there. Beatrice walked gingerly past Ophelia to her bedroom and saw an empty safe in her room. Was it a robbery then?

She glanced over at Ophelia's bedside table, spotting a library book there with what looked like a large bookmark sticking out of it. Beatrice took a tissue and opened the book. The piece of paper used as a bookmark had a list of local names on it and what appeared to be various petty infractions. She took her phone out and took a picture of the piece of paper as the sound of sirens approached. Beatrice walked outside to join Wyatt and Miss Sissy.

Ramsay looked tired as he approached the house. "People in town are really going to fuss about this," he said.

Beatrice said, "There have been two murders here before in a short period of time."

"Yes, but not on the same *day*. It makes it look as though we have some sort of serial killer in Dappled Hills on our hands, which we don't. I'm sure these crimes have got to be connected and aren't some sort of random occurrences," said Ramsay.

A state police car pulled up and Ramsay waited for the police officer before walking into the house.

Miss Sissy was sitting in Beatrice's back seat, looking rattled and hostile. She glared at Beatrice when she spotted her staring her way.

Beatrice asked Wyatt, "Is she all right?"

Wyatt sighed. "Apparently, although Miss Sissy was very annoyed with Ophelia, they were good friends. She seems really angry and upset by this, although I was able to get her calmed down a little."

"I wonder what she wanted to talk with Ophelia about," said Beatrice, frowning.

"You mean about the scene at the wedding?" asked Wyatt. "Isn't that what she was saying earlier?"

"Yes, but there was something else. She said that she wanted to speak to Ophelia about something *besides* the argument at Piper's wedding." She turned to look at Miss Sissy again. "Do you think that she would be able to talk about it?"

Wyatt shook his head. "I wouldn't try. She hasn't said a word since she found Ophelia. Well, I take it back. She did say *one* word. I asked if I could take her to the doctor, since she seemed to be in shock. And she said *no*." He paused, staring at the house. "Did you see anything out of place in there?"

Beatrice said, "It looked as though everything she owned was out of place in there. Drawers were dumped out and papers were strewn everywhere."

"Someone was looking for something, then," said Wyatt.

Beatrice said, "It certainly appears that way." She hesitated. "Ophelia's safe was open, too. It made me wonder if someone at the wedding overheard Ophelia's contention that she had tons of money and came over to take it." She shook her head. "I hate to even think that, since the wedding guests were all friends of ours."

"How many people do you think could have overheard Ophelia?" asked Wyatt.

"Plenty of people," said Beatrice with a shrug. "She was being loud, even with the band playing and everyone was moving around. Maybe ten or fifteen people? More? But something is bothering me about that. I feel almost as if this was staged. As if maybe there was another motive for someone having done this."

At this point, Ramsay came back to join them. Another state police car pulled up and more officers entered the house. Ramsay said in a low voice, "How are things over here? Miss Sissy okay?"

Wyatt said, "I think she's just in shock. Anger is gradually replacing the shock, though, which is probably a good thing. She didn't want to see a doctor. It looks like she and Ophelia were better friends than I realized."

Ramsay nodded, glancing at Miss Sissy. Then he turned to Beatrice. "What did you make of the house?"

"Well, it definitely looked as though someone was trying to find something in there. That made me wonder if someone had heard Ophelia bragging last night about how she had lots of money. But it's hard for me to fathom," said Beatrice.

Ramsay raised his eyebrows. "Hard for you to fathom that someone you know is a murderer?"

"I think I've kind of gotten over *that*, since it's happened fairly frequently. No, I mean it's hard to fathom that someone I know is so hard up for cash that they'd rob and kill an old woman," said Beatrice.

Ramsay nodded. "I see what you mean. You think it was a cover? For something else?"

"I'm not sure. But I did find something." Beatrice saw Ramsay open his mouth to scold her and quickly added, "Don't worry, I didn't disturb anything and I used a tissue to touch things. But there's a piece of paper in Ophelia's library book on her bedside table. It looks like some sort of a master list of people's wrongdoings. At any rate, it's worth a look."

"Any names you recognized?" asked Ramsay.

"Yes. Barton Perry's name was on there. And the name of someone I've heard about, but don't actually personally know: Mae Thigpen. There were a bunch of other names, but I wasn't familiar with them," said Beatrice.

Ramsay then got a formal statement from them all, although Miss Sissy's was mostly populated by grunts and silence.

An officer came out and called to Ramsay and he said, "You're all welcome to go. You must be exhausted, even though it's still early in the day. I know that I am." He walked into Ophelia's house.

Beatrice climbed into the front seat and said, "Miss Sissy, are you sure that you're all right to go back home? Would you like us to take you to see a doctor?"

"*No.*"

Beatrice and Wyatt exchanged glances. Wyatt said under his breath, "I'm not sure she needs to go back to her house and be alone."

Beatrice's head started pounding at the thought of hosting Miss Sissy all day at their tiny cottage. "Miss Sissy, would you like to come over to our house for a while? I'm not doing anything all that interesting, but you're welcome to come."

The old woman glared at her and shook her head fiercely.

Wyatt said, "What about the Patchwork Cottage? Would you like to hang out there today?" He looked at his watch. "It's not open very long on Sundays, but it should be open now."

Beatrice beamed at him. "That's a great idea! I'm sure Posy wouldn't mind. Then you can curl up in a chair with Maisie." Maisie was the beautiful white shop cat at the quilting store. Miss Sissy was Maisie's co-owner with Posy.

Miss Sissy perked up a bit, tilting her head to one side to consider this. "Okay."

"Perfect!" Beatrice practically sang the word out in her relief.

First, Beatrice dropped Wyatt off at the church office so that he could get some work done (it was a short walk from the church to their cottage). Then she drove to the Patchwork Cottage with Miss Sissy. She was relieved that the old woman's stony silence was gradually being replaced by some light humming.

A few minutes later, the two women were walking through the door at the Patchwork Cottage. Beatrice could understand why Miss Sissy felt so much cheerier at the prospect of coming here. The whole shop was relaxing with soft music piping through it, usually the work of local artists. Quilts hung from the ceiling and the walls gave the shop a soft, welcoming appearance. There were cozy chairs and a sofa in a sitting area in the middle of the store and Miss Sissy made a beeline for the sofa and the cat curled up there. When the cat spotted the old woman, she stood up, stretched, yawned, and immediately curled back up again, this time in Miss Sissy's lap.

Posy, the shop owner, greeted Beatrice with a smile. "Beatrice! Good to see you and Miss Sissy today. How is everything?"

Beatrice said in a low voice, "Actually, everything could be better. For once I'm glad to see that the store is so quiet. Is it all right for Miss Sissy to stay here today? Could you keep an eye on her in between customers? I'll warn you that she's had a bit of a shock."

Posy's bright blue eyes clouded. "Of course ... I'm happy to have her here. But whatever happened? How could anything have happened in such a short period of time? We were just with you last night at the wedding."

"I know, it seems unbelievable. As hard as it is to believe, there have been two murders this morning, Posy. I'm surprised that my phone isn't ringing like crazy with Meadow on the other end—I suppose Ramsay must not have filled her in yet. Wyatt and I were picking up a wedding present for Piper at Pearl's house and Barton came around from the backyard and told us that she was dead."

Posy gasped. Then the two women both turned as the doorbell jangled noisily as someone entered the store. It was Savannah and Georgia. They saw Beatrice and rushed over with smiles on their faces.

Georgia said, "It was the sweetest wedding ever, Beatrice!"

"Besides your own, you mean?" asked Beatrice teasingly. "I seem to remember a recent special day that was pretty high on the sweet scale."

Georgia laughed. "It *was* a great day, wasn't it? Even though it was much smaller than Piper's."

"But beautiful. You couldn't have picked a better day for a barbeque reception outdoors. I'm just amazed how lucky both you and Piper were with the weather for your wedding days. How is married life treating you so far?" asked Beatrice.

She noticed that Posy was giving Savannah worried sideways glances. Then Savannah quietly slipped away and started browsing through the shop.

Georgia said, "It's been great, but so crazy. This is the first time I've seen Savannah in ages, besides Piper's wedding. Well, *you* know, Beatrice, what being a newlywed is like! Combining two households into one is tough. And, since we bought a new house to share, we've been trying to sell Tony's house."

"That *is* a lot to adjust to. Somehow I've been so caught up in my own busyness that I missed that you and Tony had bought a house," said Beatrice.

"Well, we wanted a slightly bigger place," said Georgia with a smile. "We're hoping to have children—not right away, but before long." Her smile faded a little. "The only problem is that we have all these expenses. We hoped Tony's house might sell before now, but apparently it's too small for most of the market. And Tony's back in school, and the cost of classes and books is really adding up."

Beatrice said, "Oh, I didn't realize he was back in school. Is he still working at the hardware store during the day?"

"He is, and then he goes to school at night at the community college in Lenoir. He's trying to learn computer programming," said Georgia. "Tony wanted to get a job that would earn him more money before we tried to have a family."

"The downside is that you're probably not seeing very much of each other?" guessed Beatrice.

"Exactly! But we're hoping it will all be worth it in the end. Between my teaching and selling pet clothes online and his work and studies, we're not able to spend as much time together as we'd like," said Georgia. "Anyway, back to Piper's wedding. It was perfect in every way, Beatrice. I know she's going to be so happy with Ash."

Beatrice said, "I know she will be, too. And thanks about the wedding—it does feel like a dream. Especially in light of a very unsettling morning."

Savannah rejoined their group and she and Georgia frowned at Posy's and Beatrice's solemn expression. "What's happened?" asked Georgia.

Beatrice started repeating what she'd told Posy when suddenly the doorbell jangled once again. This time they turned to see Meadow there.

Meadow said, "Well, I'm glad to see all of you! I've been bored to tears at home all morning. Ramsay left the house early and he's not been answering his phone—it's most annoying!" She noticed their faces and said, "All right. What's happened?"

Beatrice filled them in on both the incident at the reception and the two murders that morning, while the women stared, stunned, at her.

"How did Barton take the news?" asked Georgia, a frown furrowing her brow.

Beatrice said, "He seemed completely shocked. And almost disbelieving. When he'd left the house to drive off to the gym, Pearl was heading out to do some weeding in the yard."

"Ophelia *and* Pearl are dead?" asked Posy. She shook her head.

Savannah scowled. "Makes a body not feel safe anymore."

Meadow was quite agitated at the news. "Not feel safe in Dappled Hills? This is *criminal*."

"Well, there's no doubt about that," agreed Beatrice dryly.

"What is Ramsay doing about all this?" demanded Meadow, hands on hips.

Beatrice said in a placating voice, "He's scrambling around like crazy, Meadow. That's why you haven't heard back from him today. It was as much of a surprise to Ramsay as it was to us, remember. He's working with the state police to try to find out who's behind these murders. They must somehow be connected."

Meadow frowned. "The weird thing is that Pearl and Ophelia had that argument at the reception. Remember? You'd think that one of *them* would be responsible for the death of the other. Or that maybe one of them killed the other and then took their *own* life, in guilt."

Beatrice shook her head. "There's no way that Pearl hit herself over the head with a flowerpot. Or that Ophelia hit herself over the head with a bottle of wine."

Meadow said, pursing her lips "I kept telling people that Ophelia drank. It was probably that cheap wine that I saw her buying at the grocery store. She always acted as if she was too good to drink, but I knew better."

Georgia said, "Beatrice, were there any clues at all as to who might be behind this?"

Savannah said grimly, "Now we're going to have to start locking our doors again."

Beatrice said calmly, hoping her calm would transfer to the other women, "I really don't think there's a larger threat here. There was a reason that Pearl and Ophelia were targeted, although we don't know yet what that was. I'm sure Ramsay and the state police are hot on their trail."

Meadow snorted. "I think we're better off with you poking around, Beatrice. You know that you have a real knack for this stuff. Nothing against Ramsay, or anything, but you know that he would rather be off reading his collection of Yeats than doing police work."

"I'm sure he's working very hard, Meadow." Beatrice turned to Georgia. "And, to answer your question, there were a couple of clues. Not at Pearl's house so much, but at Ophelia's. There was a list of names there."

"What sort of a list?" asked Meadow, leaning closer to Beatrice.

"It looked as though it was a list of people and their misdeeds," said Beatrice. She pulled out her phone and showed them all the picture she'd taken in Ophelia's house.

The other women read in silence.

Meadow snorted. "Most of these are minor offenses. See, this is what I was telling you about Ophelia. She got involved in other people's business. Honestly, I'm not too shocked that someone decided to murder her. She was always sneaking around, gathering gossip and looking down on everyone." She squinted at Beatrice's phone. "*Jim Jacobs littered in front of the café.* I mean, who *cares*? Ophelia just liked to think that she was better than everyone else."

Savannah asked, squinting at the phone, "It doesn't make sense. Why are most of them scratched out and a couple of them not?"

Georgia frowned. "Maybe the ones that were scratched off *were* less-important, like Meadow was saying. The ones that aren't scratched off could be more important. Or maybe the scratched-off ones were ones that she felt she'd dealt with."

Meadow raised her eyebrows. "I see that Pearl Perry's name isn't scratched off. And Pearl, of course, was trying to give Ophelia money."

"Maybe Pearl thought that she could pay Ophelia off," said Beatrice. "Somehow I couldn't see Pearl charitably handing out money to Ophelia. Giving money at a wedding reception seems like a very odd thing to have done. And they certainly didn't seem close."

"*No one* was close to Ophelia!" said Meadow.

Posy shook her head in gentle correction. "That's not entirely true, although Ophelia could be very difficult." She glanced over to where Miss Sissy was slumped over, snoring with abandon, as Maisie slept on her lap.

Beatrice nodded. "Miss Sissy was very distraught over her death."

Posy said, "I'm glad Miss Sissy is here. She didn't need to be alone today."

Meadow said, "Exactly. I bet she'll feel a lot better when she wakes up." She looked at Beatrice, "So where to, first?"

Chapter Five

"Where to?" asked Beatrice.

"Naturally, we're going to head off and investigate. We can't leave Ramsay and the state police to their own devices, can we? They need your expertise! And we need to get these murders solved before everyone is a nervous wreck and padlocking their doors all the time," said Meadow. "So where do we start out?"

Beatrice said, "Well, ordinarily I'd say that we'd want to start off with either Pearl or Ophelia, considering that there was an incident at the reception. But since both of them are dead, I'm thinking that we need to look at the bigger picture."

"Which is?" asked Georgia, looking confused.

"Why would someone want to murder both Ophelia and Pearl? And did it have something to do with their argument at the reception?" said Beatrice.

Posy absently straightened a fabric display. "Do you think that someone might have used the murder as a cover-up?"

"What do you mean?" asked Meadow. "Cover-up for what?"

Posy got a little flustered. "Oh, I don't know what I'm talking about, really. But maybe someone *wanted* to murder Ophelia, for their own reasons. And then, when it became clear that Pearl and Ophelia had had words, they decided to go ahead and murder Ophelia and maybe everyone would blame Pearl for it. Since they'd been arguing."

"That's certainly a possibility," said Beatrice. "But why kill Pearl, in that case?"

Meadow said, "Maybe they wanted to make it look as if Pearl had murdered Ophelia and then felt so guilty that she took her own life."

"Maybe," said Beatrice. "But if that was the case, then why would they so clearly murder Pearl? As I said earlier, there's no way that Pearl could have hit herself over the head with that flowerpot."

Posy sighed. "I can see this is going to take some time and some hard work to unravel."

"We need to get to work," Meadow told Beatrice urgently.

Beatrice said, "Does anyone know anything about Mae Thigpen? She's the other name on the list that's not scratched out. Her name is familiar, but I don't think I've ever met her."

"She's my neighbor," said Savannah. "Lives right next door."

"Really?" asked Beatrice, raising her eyebrows. "I don't think I've ever heard you mention her before."

Georgia said, "She's very quiet and not at all sociable. Although she's very pleasant whenever we *do* speak," she said in a hurry, never one to speak badly of others.

Meadow said to Beatrice, "Let's go over there."

"Unannounced? What are we supposed to do, demand to know if she had anything to do with Pearl's and Ophelia's deaths?" asked Beatrice. "I haven't even been properly introduced to her."

"We could tell her that we're collecting for charity," said Meadow breezily. "We'll knock on the door and ask for a donation for the Red Cross or some such. Then I'll just mail it over to them so it won't even be a lie."

Beatrice shook her head. "We've done that before. I don't think it was a great excuse because to get anywhere with it, we had to act as though we desperately needed to have a drink of water or use the restroom or something to get inside the house. Otherwise, they'd just give us a couple of dollars and shut the door on us."

Georgia said brightly, "I know! Mae leaves her house every day when she walks her little dog. At least, she did when I was still living there."

Savannah nodded thoughtfully. "That's right. And she still does, too. What kind of dog is it? A chihuahua?"

"No, I think it's a Pekingese, isn't it? At any rate, Mae seems to be very routine-driven and takes him at the same time every day: two o'clock. You could run over to the house and be there when she leaves," said Georgia. "Maybe you could have a few words before she heads out. You could say you were there visiting Savannah."

Savannah said, "Wouldn't it be better to go over to where she *walks* the dog? They'd have more time that way."

"Does she work from home, then?" asked Meadow. "How is she able to always leave at two?"

Georgia said slowly, "I don't really know a lot about her, but I've heard that she has some family money. She's widowed, and I think her husband's death left her comfortable."

"Probably a life insurance policy," said Savannah approvingly. "Smart man."

"Anyway, she works at home doing some sort of computer-related stuff," said Georgia. "So it's not as if she's unemployed. But the money she had from her husband's death appears to be supplementing her income."

Beatrice said, "Where does she usually walk the dog? In your neighborhood?"

Georgia's face fell. "No, she always gets in her car with him. Oh, dear. I didn't think about that. Where on earth do they go? There are lots of places around Dappled Hills to walk a dog."

Savannah said briskly, "Well, I know exactly where she walks him. I've been riding my bicycle when I've seen her putting the Pekinese in or out of the car at the park."

"The big park? Where the reception was?" asked Beatrice. "The one next door to Pearl's house?"

"The very one," said Savannah with a bob of her head.

"All right, let's go!" said Meadow energetically. She was so energetic that she startled Maisie, who startled Miss Sissy. Both the cat and the old woman glared at her before they quickly dropped back to sleep.

"We should make it more believable by taking a dog with us," said Beatrice dryly. "If Mae goes to the park to walk her dog each day, she'll know that she's never seen *us* there before."

"What? You and I are very active people, Beatrice. We go to the park all the time," said Meadow indignantly.

"Do we? I usually walk in the neighborhood. I may take Noo-noo to the park sometimes, but not every day. And not when I'm asking a lot of nosy questions about a murder to someone I don't know," said Beatrice.

Meadow didn't appear to be listening. "We can take Boris with us! He hasn't had a walk in the last few days. The poor dog must be dying to get out."

"The problem with taking Boris is, that we don't walk him. *He* walks *us*," said Beatrice. "That can't be the best way to have a conversation with anyone."

"Okay, you're probably right. He won't be any better with having had no walk recently, either. Let's run by and pick up Noo-noo then. I'll take my Boris on a solo walk later," said Meadow.

Posy said, "Do be careful, please. With two deaths already, I'm feeling very anxious."

Georgia said, "And if you find out something, let Ramsay deal with it. There's no point in putting yourselves in danger."

Beatrice nodded, "We'll be very discreet, won't we, Meadow?"

Meadow, of course, looked like the least-discreet person around. But she bobbed her head in agreement. "We'll be so careful that no one will even realize that we're investigating." She paused for a moment and said hesitantly in a rather unconvincing voice, "Oh, wait. There's something I needed here. I forgot." She disappeared into the fabrics while Georgia and Savannah quickly checked out and said their goodbyes.

As soon as the bell rang indicating that the two sisters had left, Meadow emerged from behind a display of fat quarters. "They're both gone?" she asked in her stage whisper.

Beatrice and Posy nodded and Meadow hurried over. "Okay. So Posy, what's the scoop? I thought I remembered whatever you wanted to tell me had something to do with Savannah. It's okay to speak in front of Beatrice, right? Since she's *family* now!" She gave Beatrice one of her emotional smiles that always made Beatrice nervous that Meadow would explode into happy tears again.

Posy said, "Oh, of course. I just didn't mention it to Beatrice because I know how busy mothers of brides can be. I've just been worried about Savannah, that's all. And, naturally, she looked like her old self today, right as I've been worrying day and night! So maybe I've been stewing over nothing."

Beatrice shook her head. "I wouldn't say that Savannah was one hundred percent her old self. She disappeared when Georgia was telling us about her married life."

Meadow frowned. "That's true. I thought that was sort of odd."

Posy said, "That's just the thing. As Georgia was mentioning, there's just no time in her day for really *anything*. Probably not even for a good night's sleep. And, unfortunately, not so much time for her sister." She hurried on, "Which is completely understandable! After all, she has so much on her plate."

Beatrice mused, "And Savannah doesn't have very much on hers."

"And they lived together for all those years!" said Meadow. "Spending so much of their lives together. Georgia always used to watch out for Savannah, too."

Posy said, "It's not as if Savannah is *totally* alone. She does have Smoke."

"But having a cat isn't exactly the same," said Beatrice.

Meadow said sadly, "Her friends haven't even had very much time for her lately, either. What with the weddings and all, I've barely had time to even shove food down my throat a few times a day." She reached out for Beatrice. "We have to start hanging out with Savannah!"

Beatrice said, "But is that the best solution to the problem? I don't think Savannah wants us to spend time with her because we feel as though we *need* to."

Posy said, "I was hoping that maybe she could spend more time here at the shop. She could do some quilting and visit with the customers who come through."

There was a snore behind them and Beatrice said wryly, "Quilting and visiting at the shop? Sounds like Miss Sissy. Except for the visiting part."

Meadow said with relief, "That's a great idea, Posy. And she could hang out with Miss Sissy!"

It seemed to be very important to Meadow that Savannah *hang out* with someone. Beatrice said, "But is Miss Sissy fun to sit with all day? Besides, it doesn't sound as though that's something that Savannah is interested in doing." Beatrice glanced at her watch. "Meadow, we should head on if we're going to catch up with Mae during her dog walk. Let's just all mull over Savannah. Maybe a solution will present itself to us. And, in the meantime, maybe we can all find a little extra time to visit with her or drop by or something."

A minute later, Beatrice and Meadow hopped into their respective cars. Meadow rolled down her window. "How about if I just meet you at the park instead of following you home and then going? We're getting very close to two o'clock and I just don't want to miss Mae in case she comes a bit early."

"Sounds good," said Beatrice and she drove back home rather quickly. At least this time she didn't have Miss Sissy scowling at her and complaining about her driving. Soon she was back home, putting a harness and leash on Noo-noo, and hurrying back out to the car.

Noo-noo was delighted to be going for a ride and grinned out of the window the whole way there, lifting her nose to better smell the mountain air. When she saw that they were at the park, her little nubbin of a tail started wagging excitedly. Beatrice pulled into a spot next to Meadow's car.

Meadow rolled her window down. "Mae hasn't gotten here yet."

They heard a car pull in on the gravel behind them and turned.

"Is that Mae?" asked Beatrice.

Meadow said, "It sure is. She must have left her house at two o'clock on the dot." She pushed open her car door with vigor.

"Now Meadow, we need to make sure we're subtle about this. It sounds as though Mae might be shy or something," said Beatrice in a cautious tone.

Meadow snorted. "She's not a bit shy. She's merely introverted. Mae doesn't really want to be around people, that's all."

Beatrice felt as though she and Mae may have quite a bit in common.

"All right, well, let's still give her some space. Let's take Noo-noo on down the path while she's getting her Pekingese out of the car. Then we can pause and let Mae catch up to us. Otherwise, it makes it appear as if we're lying in wait for her."

"Which is exactly what we're doing," said Meadow with a chuckle.

Beatrice helped Noo-noo get out of the car and the little dog immediately started slowly walking while sniffing at all the fascinating smells on the ground.

"Mae will catch up easily at this rate," said Meadow with a laugh. "You're right about Boris. He'd have pulled us half a mile down the trail by this point."

A sharp ring started emanating from Beatrice's pocket, making her jump. She fumbled with the leash and Meadow took it away from her. Beatrice glanced at the unfamiliar local number. "Hello?" she muttered inhospitably.

"Beatrice Coleman?" The younger woman's voice sounded hectic.

"This is she," said Beatrice cautiously.

"Oh, good. I just drove to the church to take my son to the church basketball team practice and no one was there. Clearly, the schedule has changed and I didn't hear about it. Do you know when the practice is now?" asked the woman. She then said, "Your water's in the backseat, Grayson. Yes, it is! Don't argue with me, young man."

Beatrice watched as Mae got her small dog out of the car. "I'm afraid I have no idea when the game is."

"It's *not* a game, it's a practice. It's the one for the 8-10-year-old boys. Don't you know?" The woman's voice was irritated.

Beatrice said coolly, "I'm afraid if it's not on the church calendar, I wouldn't have any idea."

"Do you think your husband would know?" asked the woman persistently.

"I doubt it. You should call the team coach," said Beatrice in a rush as Mae started walking in their direction.

"I did, but I couldn't get him," said the woman, who still seemed to be fielding water bottles and snacks in her car.

"Perhaps another parent on the team?" asked Beatrice, gritting her teeth a bit.

"I suppose I could. I think I have the parent list somewhere," said the woman, in a put-out voice."

"That would be the way to go. Thanks for calling," said Beatrice in what she feared was a rather insincere voice. She hung up with a sigh.

Meadow handed her back the leash. "Wow. Do you get many calls like that? How is the minister's wife supposed to know the intimate details of the 8-10 year old boys' basketball practices?"

"I guess you overheard. Yes, actually, I have gotten a lot of calls, mostly in the last week. It's a small church, but it's incredibly active and I can't keep up. I have the church calendar app on my phone now, but that doesn't help me if the event isn't on the calendar or got rescheduled or something. It's very frustrating," said Beatrice.

Meadow said, "That's probably because they printed your cell number in the bulletin."

Beatrice froze. "Who? Who are 'they'? And when did this happen?"

"About a week ago. I guess the church officers? I'm sure Wyatt wouldn't have done it—he doesn't think the minister's wife is supposed to have an unpaid role, I know," said Meadow.

Beatrice said, "It's just because we lost the church secretary. She knew *everything* about *everything*. Now we can't keep up. There's no one at the church office answering phones. Maybe the officers thought it was a good short-term solution. In the meantime, I'm unfortunately just going to sound as if I have no idea what's going on. Because I don't. Look, here she comes."

Noo-noo started sniffing earnestly in the grass off the side of the path. A woman in her forties with red hair and beautiful porcelain skin walked up with her dog. She gave them a brief smile but didn't seem at all inclined to stop and talk.

Meadow leaped into action. "Mae Thigpen!" she cried out in a jolly voice. "Wow, I haven't seen you for a while—how have you been?" She walked up to Mae and threw her arms around her in an effusive hug, effectively tackling her. Mae made an *oof* as the wind got knocked out of her. Beatrice had to hand it to Meadow—Mae was stopped in her tracks in a most efficient manner.

Mae looked longingly down the path for a second, then resolutely turned to give another quick smile to Meadow and Beatrice. "I've been doing well, just working from home."

Meadow said, "I'd be remiss in saying how sorry I was to hear about the terrible news. Poor Ophelia."

Beatrice glared at Meadow. That was hardly a subtle opener. And why on earth would Mae care about Ophelia, if she even knew who the old woman was? It sounded as if Mae spent most of her day inside, which is why Beatrice hadn't met her.

Mae gave Meadow a sharp look and then said in a subdued voice, "Yes, that was terrible news, wasn't it?" But it didn't sound as though she was at all convinced that it was, in fact, terrible at all.

Meadow said, "Oh, heavens, I forgot to introduce you to my friend. Mae, this is Beatrice Coleman. Oops! I mean Beatrice Thompson. I can't seem to get used to the married name. Beatrice, Mae Thigpen. Beatrice is Wyatt's new wife. I know we go to the same church."

They shook hands. Mae's handshake was firm and brisk as if she'd steeled herself for the contact. She clearly wasn't trying to make friends. The two dogs, on the other hand, seemed to be making each other's acquaintance.

Meadow said to Beatrice, "Mae is Ophelia's niece. *Was* her niece."

"Great-niece, actually," corrected Mae smoothly.

"I'm so sorry for your loss," said Beatrice. And she was especially sorry that Meadow hadn't explained that Mae and Ophelia were related before this conversation started. But then, half the residents of Dappled Hills seemed to be somehow related to everyone else.

Mae shifted a bit uncomfortably. "Thank you. I'm afraid, though, that Aunt Ophelia and I weren't all that close. She generally disapproved of me."

Meadow said, "Surely not! What on earth for?"

"Oh, I think she thought my drinking was inappropriate." She gave a small laugh. "Mind you, she drank herself, although she'd never admit it. All I have is a glass of wine to unwind at the end of the day, but Aunt Ophelia thought it was wicked," Mae's lips curled into a faintly amused smile.

"Did you see each other often?" asked Beatrice. "Of course, in such a small town, I'd imagine that you'd see her out running errands, too. Did she also drop by for visits?"

"Not as infrequently as I would have liked. Our typical visits would entail her rapping on my door loudly enough to wake the dead. I'd answer the door and she'd stride right to the refrigerator and yank it open. There would be an open bottle of white wine in there and she'd start shaking her head and throwing all sorts of dire statements my way. I'd reluctantly ask her if she wanted to sit down, and she'd plop down on my sofa and start telling me all sorts of horrid gossip about other people in the town. It made me very aware that she was likely spreading tales about me, too," said Mae.

Mae's features were hard as she talked about her aunt, but when her little dog jumped up and put his legs on hers as if to encourage her to walk, her face softened. "We'll walk in a minute, Bizzy."

"Had you seen her recently?" asked Beatrice. She reached down and petted Bizzy, who had bumped her leg with her nose.

"Maybe she'd seen *me*, but I hadn't seen her. Aunt Ophelia came to my house last week, but I pretended not to be home. And, before you ask, I was at home when my aunt was murdered. I've already told the police that, when asked. Bizzy is my alibi," said Mae wryly.

Bizzy looked adoringly at Mae like, if she could only understand what Mae was saying, she would be more than happy to do anything she wanted.

Beatrice flushed a little. "I'm sorry, I must seem very nosy."

Meadow said, "You're *not* nosy. You simply have a gift for figuring out these kinds of cases. You're a gifted amateur."

"Do you know of anyone who might want to harm your aunt?" asked Beatrice.

Mae gave a short laugh. "Besides everyone, you mean?"

"Anyone specific?" pressed Beatrice.

"I did happen to spot my aunt last week when I was on my way to a dental appointment. She appeared to be yelling at Violet Louise right in downtown Dappled Hills." Mae gave an expressive shrug as if to say it was business as usual for Ophelia.

Meadow gaped at Mae. "In the middle of town? What on earth was she yelling at poor Violet about?"

"Who knows? I was simply trying to make sure that my aunt didn't spot me and try to make conversation with me. Otherwise, I'd have ended up her next victim. I hurried on down the sidewalk and walked into the dental office," said Mae.

Beatrice asked, "If the police have already spoken with you, you must have also heard about Pearl's death."

Mae's lips tightened and she nodded. "I certainly did. Now *that's* a shock. I don't think I've ever heard anyone in town say anything negative about Pearl."

"So no ideas who might have been behind her death?" asked Beatrice.

"None whatsoever," said Mae. "As opposed to my aunt's death. I would think there would be plenty of prospects there, as I've already mentioned."

Beatrice said, "What was Violet's reaction when your aunt was yelling at her?"

"Violet looked none too pleased. Maybe she was angry enough to go to my aunt's house and confront her about the matter." Mae shrugged.

"But why would *anyone* have a problem with Violet Louise?" asked Meadow.

Mae shrugged again, looking annoyed. "How would I know? Maybe the argument and my aunt's murder are totally unrelated things. Isn't that for you to find out? I'm supposed to be the one supplying information and then Beatrice is supposed to figure out how it all fits together ... right?"

Beatrice took a deep breath, trying to keep from firing back at Mae. Mae must have realized how she sounded, because she sounded more reconciliatory when she spoke again.

"I'm sorry. It's been a very strange day. And ... did I hear that my aunt was also robbed?"

Beatrice and Meadow nodded.

Mae said, "I do know that Violet doesn't have two cents to rub together. Maybe that's part of her motive. But I really don't think that I know anything else that could help you." She again looked longingly down the path. "Well, I'll leave you to it. Good luck to you, Beatrice. Especially with Pearl's death. Now *that* was tragic. Nice to meet you."

And, with a little word of encouragement to Bizzy, she strode off down the path.

Chapter Six

Meadow looked after them in frustration. "That was completely unproductive."

"On the contrary, I think we acquired some excellent information. Mae was no fan of her aunt and her aunt was no fan of hers. And Ophelia had a public argument with Violet Louise. By the way, you could have told me at the very beginning that Mae and Ophelia were related."

Meadow looked blankly at her. "But I figured you knew. Half the town is related to each other, anyway."

"Yes, in some general cousinly way. But this is fairly direct. Is *Violet Louise* related to anyone I should know about?" asked Beatrice. "And let's start walking. Poor Noo-noo is wondering what we're doing out here if we're not going to walk."

"At least we won't catch up with Mae since she's practically galloping down the path. To answer your question, no, Violet isn't related to anyone remotely associated with these murders. I don't think I can believe a word out of Mae Thigpen's mouth. She was in such a brusque mood! I think she'd have told us anything to get rid of us," said Meadow. "Besides, Violet is one of our quilting sisters."

"Oh, I see. I know how you feel about fellow quilters. In your opinion, they're always trustworthy and of too sterling a character to possibly be able to break the law," said Beatrice.

Meadow laughed. "Am I that obvious? But it's true, isn't it? I'd believe whatever Violet Louise had to say before I listened to Mae. Besides, what could the two of them be arguing about?"

"I don't know, but I'm not completely inclined to disbelieve Mae. I'm sure she was right about the fact that she avoided her aunt, for instance. What do you know about Violet? All I know is that she's in the Cut-Ups guild and that she's fairly young for a quilter," said Beatrice.

Meadow said, "She's such a promising quilter, Beatrice. She's already won a couple of shows and she's only been quilting for a year or so. You're correct about her age—she's around thirty, I think." She made a face. "The Cut-Ups have somehow done a really stellar job recruiting new members."

Beatrice raised her eyebrows. "Really? That's unusual. Ordinarily, *you're* the one who is rushing potential members. I seem to remember that I was practically kidnapped when I first moved to Dappled Hills and conscripted into membership with the Village Quilters."

"Yes, but I was simply saving you time! You'd have decided to join the guild anyway. Why not cut to the chase?" said Meadow with a shrug.

Beatrice said dryly, "You've obviously decided on different tactics if the Cut-Ups are growing their membership."

Meadow sighed. "I've just been busy, that's all. I've been all tied up with Piper and Ash's wedding. While that planning was going on, the Cut-Ups managed to recruit both Violet and Edgenora."

"Edgenora?" asked Beatrice, raising her eyebrows.

"Yes. She recently moved to Dappled Hills because she said the winters were too cold where she was from," said Meadow.

"Where was she from?" asked Beatrice. "I think the winters are pretty cold here in the mountains."

"Buffalo, New York," said Meadow with a smile.

"Ah. Yes, we're fairly tropical in comparison," said Beatrice.

"You know, you don't really hear names like Edgenora so much anymore," said Meadow thoughtfully.

"Thank goodness," said Beatrice.

"It's hard to imagine anyone naming their baby Edgenora. Can you imagine? Anyway, she seems nice. She has a sort of stern personality, but she's friendly enough. I've only met her briefly a couple of times in the Patchwork Cottage. Posy was helping her buy a bunch of quilting supplies to get started with."

Noo-noo stopped to smell something on the side of the path again, and then looked quickly behind her as if suspecting they'd have another long delay in the walk if she loitered too long. She started trotting and Beatrice and Meadow picked up their paces.

"Going back to Violet, do you have any ideas about how I might go about asking her some questions?" asked Beatrice.

"I still say she couldn't be involved. But I'm sure quilting would be the perfect excuse." Meadow's voice was a little breathless from the faster pace.

"It's not as if I can infiltrate a Cut-Ups guild meeting," said Beatrice.

"No, but you're likely to see her at the Patchwork Cottage," said Meadow.

"Only if I spend all of my time there, which I don't have time to do. In fact, I'd planned on spending more time at the church this week. I'm still trying to figure out how to get more involved there and what sort of role I want to have," said Beatrice. "Except, *not* as unofficial church secretary."

Meadow snapped her fingers, which made Noo-noo turn around expectantly. "Sorry, Noo-noo. I was just remembering that Violet was talking about the church, herself." Noo-noo turned back around and kept trotting.

"She goes to Wyatt's church?" asked Beatrice in surprise. "Somehow I didn't realize that. Although I'll admit to having a hard time learning all the members of the congregation."

"Violet is a member, all right. So, if you can wait until Sunday, that might be a good time to catch up with her." Meadow gave a short laugh. "Speaking of catching up, I thought we took Noo-noo because Boris was going to make us have to run behind him. Noo-noo has turned into a personal trainer!"

"We're jogging today, for sure," said Beatrice with a breathless laugh. "I think she was taken aback by the length of time we spent talking to Mae. When we go out for a walk, especially at the park, she expects a walk!

"And so she should!" said Meadow emphatically. "I only wish I'd put my running shoes on." She snapped her fingers. "I know what I meant to tell you today. I was going to tell you in the Patchwork Cottage, but then it flew out of my head as soon as I heard about poor Pearl and Ophelia."

"What is it?" asked Beatrice with more than a little bit of apprehension. Frequently, Meadow's excitement over something meant that Beatrice was going to need to sacrifice some of her free time.

"Don't look so worried! Just remember that we have a guild meeting day after tomorrow, that's all."

They gave Noo-noo another fifteen minutes of exercise and then parted ways in the park's parking lot. Meadow tooted her horn as she left and rolled down her window to say, "I'll pump Ramsay for more information. We need more leads than just Mae and Violet." Then she drove off at her usual madcap speed.

Beatrice glanced at the clock in her car. "Let's stop by and see Wyatt, Noo-noo." It was the very middle of the afternoon and she knew that Wyatt liked to have a little snack around now to tide him over until supper. She dug her cell phone from her pocket.

"June Bug? It's Beatrice. I was thinking about dropping by to pick up a couple of muffins from you, but I have Noo-noo in the car. Is there any way you could run them out to me and I could pay you?"

June Bug said, "Oh yes. Katy is here and she could run it out to you."

"That would be perfect! She'll be like one of the old-timey carhops," said Beatrice.

A few minutes later, Beatrice parked in front of June Bug's bakery. June Bug gave a quick wave through the window and then her young niece, Katy, came half-skipping out. It looked as though Katy might be having a mid-afternoon snack too, since there was evidence of chocolate around her mouth. Beatrice thought that a bakery would be an excellent place to hang out if one was a child.

Katy delivered the bag of muffins with a grin that revealed a couple of missing teeth. Beatrice smiled back at her. "Thanks for the muffins! Has the tooth fairy visited your house recently?"

Katy's eyes grew as big as her smile. "She took my teeth from a special pillow that June Bug made and left me money! And the money had fairy dust on it!" She reached in and rubbed Noo-noo who nuzzled her hand.

Beatrice said, "That's amazing!"

They chatted a few more minutes before Katy gave Noo-noo a final pat and skipped back inside the bakery. Beatrice drove off to the church. Wyatt's office at the church had a small patio behind it. It was beautiful outside and she thought that she and Wyatt could share their snack out there. Fortunately, she'd brought along some treats for Noo-noo, too.

Beatrice parked in front of the old church, which seemed to blend in with the nature around it with its moss-covered old stones and ivy climbing up the walls. It was surrounded by large, flowering bushes and the trees overhead created a canopy for the sun to peek through. She was getting Noo-noo out of the car when she heard a voice behind her.

"What an adorable little dog! May I pet her?"

Beatrice turned and paused in confusion. Wasn't this Violet Louise? She'd always been bad with names and learning so many of them recently had been a challenge. Was it just because she and Meadow had been talking about her?

Beatrice said, "Of course! This is Noo-noo."

For the next few minutes, the woman crooned over Noo-noo, who was positively preening over the attention. The woman was about thirty years old with straight brown hair and heavy eyebrows. Her clothing was clean but definitely old, as the edges of her shirt around her wrists were fraying.

Beatrice said, "I think we've met, but I'm terrible with names. I'm Beatrice Thompson."

The young woman smiled up at her, still stooped over Noo-noo. "Oh, I know. You're the minister's wife. It's good to meet you. I'm Violet Louise." She stood reluctantly up and shook Beatrice's hand.

Now Beatrice realized that she *had* seen Violet quite a few times at the services lately. It appeared that she'd suddenly started spending more time at the church. Of course, the same could be said for Beatrice, but Violet hadn't married a minister.

Violet said, "I was just finishing helping with the church nursery. I sometimes work there for a little extra income. There's an exercise class that meets in the gym and I watch the kids for the moms."

This sounded familiar to Beatrice now that she thought of it. Although, the exercise class had definitely not been on her list of things to investigate for more church involvement. "I'm sure they appreciate the help," she said quickly. She hesitated. "I wonder if there's something that I could ask you about. You see, I've just been very concerned about these terrible crimes lately."

Violet, who had stooped to rub Noo-noo again, gave Beatrice a slightly nervous look. "You mean the murder? Ophelia's death?"

"And Pearl's, too, of course," said Beatrice.

Violet's mouth opened in surprise. "Pearl? Pearl Perry? But I didn't hear about her murder. How awful!" Her brow wrinkled in distress.

"I'm surprised that you didn't, in a town this size," said Beatrice.

"Well, I guess I've been keeping myself busy at the church lately," said Violet, with a frown.

"I'm surprised that you didn't hear about it from someone at the church," said Beatrice. "After all, the church kitchen has been making casseroles for Barton and that kind of thing. Anyway, I've been trying to work out how they could have happened. I was speaking to someone a little while ago and they mentioned that you might have had a run-in with Ophelia shortly before her death. I thought you could maybe help me figure out what Ophelia's frame of mind was at the time. Could you share some light on it at all?" asked Beatrice, trying to look like a mere concerned citizen.

Violet gave a short laugh. "I only wish that I *could* shed light on it. She was crazy. That's the only takeaway for me. Ophelia was driving behind me and saw me not come to a full stop at a stop sign. I guess it was more of a rolling stop. Anyway, she started yelling at me right in downtown Dappled Hills. It was very upsetting." A red flush climbed up Violet's neck, just thinking about it. She nuzzled at Noo-noo as if trying to calm herself down with the soft little dog. Noo-noo nuzzled her back.

"What was your response to Ophelia?" asked Beatrice.

"My response? Oh, I just walked away. At least, I tried to. She kept following me and screeching." Violet shuddered. "At least it wasn't a very busy time of the day or else the whole town would have been talking about it. As you said, 'a town this size.'"

"It's one of those things where you always remember where you were when it happened," said Beatrice.

Violet nodded. "This morning I was part of the church bake sale when all that was happening. Although I didn't hear about the deaths there."

Beatrice blinked. As a matter of fact, she did recall that the church was having a bake sale. She'd thought about taking part in it, but then realized that baking was never her forte, nor was making change at the register. And, besides, it was right after Piper's wedding. Beatrice seemed to remember that Posy had signed up—she'd have to ask her about it. Posy must have been there before she opened up the shop for the day.

"Can you think of anyone who might have done such a thing? To either Ophelia or Pearl?" asked Beatrice.

Violet quickly said, "Well, I don't like to speak ill of the dead."

She already had, though, in her depictions of her confrontation with Ophelia.

Violet continued, "Let's face it—Ophelia wasn't easy to get along with. I can't imagine that I'm the only person who had a run-in with her. As a matter of fact, Ophelia did say something kind of odd when she was yelling at me," said Violet thoughtfully. "I was barely listening to her because I kept looking around to make sure there wasn't a crowd gathering in downtown Dappled Hills to stare at us."

"What did she say?" asked Beatrice.

"Ophelia compared me to Lois Lee," said Violet with a shrug. "I have no idea what that means, even. But I figure it must mean that she has *something* on Lois ... that Lois did something wrong in Ophelia's eyes. As for Pearl, I have no idea. She was always very polite and gracious whenever I saw her. I'm really surprised that anyone would do something like that."

Violet gave Noo-noo one final rub and then reluctantly said, "I guess I should be heading on my way. Be careful out there, Beatrice." Then she headed off to an older model small car that was in dire need of a paint job and drove away.

Chapter Seven

Wyatt was, indeed, ready for a snack. Beatrice found him in his book-covered office and it was easy to lure him out to the patio to pet Noo-noo and enjoy the muffins. There was a soft breeze rippling through the bushes and trees and it was lovely to be surrounded by nature on the small patio.

"How is everything going?" asked Wyatt. He grimaced. "I think I'll be turning in early tonight after the shocks we experienced this morning."

Beatrice said slowly, "It's all going well. Miss Sissy was napping soundly when I left the Patchwork Cottage—she'd agree with you about the exhaustion relating to shock. Posy was keeping an eye on her. Then Meadow and I took Noo-noo out to the park for a walk."

Wyatt raised his eyebrows. "You did? I know that's not part of your usual routine with her. She must have loved it."

"She did. But there was something of an ulterior motive, because Savannah and Georgia told me that Mae Thigpen always walks her dog at two o'clock there," said Beatrice. She took a bite of a moist banana nut muffin.

"Mae Thigpen being interesting because of Ophelia?" asked Wyatt.

"That's right. Ophelia had written her name down on that list of hers. I hadn't realized the connection between the two of them, either," said Beatrice. "I didn't know that Ophelia was Mae's aunt."

Wyatt said, "Unfortunately, there wasn't *that* much of a connection between them. That is, they're related by blood, but they were never very close. I think that Ophelia, in particular, would have liked a closer relationship to Mae."

Beatrice nodded. "Mae didn't have many kind words for Ophelia, that's for sure. She said that Ophelia dropped by her house even though Mae didn't exactly make her feel welcome. And that Ophelia disapproved of her because she drank."

Wyatt smiled. "That's a bit ironic. I don't believe that Ophelia was a teetotaler, herself."

"She wasn't—at least, that's what Meadow said. And then there was the murder weapon," said Beatrice. "I'd imagine that the wine bottle was handy for the murderer and not brought in by the killer."

"Did Mae give you any other leads?" asked Wyatt.

"She said that Ophelia had quarreled with Violet Louise in the middle of Dappled Hills," said Beatrice. "And on my way into the church, I saw Violet on her way out."

Wyatt said, "She's been at the church quite a bit recently. Not only has her attendance grown on Sundays, but I think she's been helping out a lot with different activities."

"And helping watch the kids in the nursery, too, apparently. It sounded as if part of it is to make some extra money, but part of it is also that she wants to be here and helping out." Beatrice thought about this for a moment as she finished up her muffin. "She said that Ophelia was yelling at her for not coming to a complete stop at a stop sign."

Wyatt sighed. "That sounds likely to me. Ophelia did seem to be tracking various people's indiscretions over the last five years or so. When I'd visit with her, she'd spend much of our visit trying to give a complete outline of everyone's sins while I unsuccessfully tried redirecting her. It was a real obsession of hers."

"No wonder she wasn't very popular in town," said Beatrice dryly. "Violet also mentioned that Ophelia had compared her to Lois Lee and that Lois may have had some sort of run-in with Ophelia. At least it doesn't appear to have been at Piper and Ash's reception."

"So I suppose that Lois is going to be getting a visit from you, soon?" asked Wyatt with a smile.

"Actually, I'm going to give her a call after I leave because I have an excellent excuse. Piper had borrowed Lois's punchbowl for the reception and tasked me with returning it to her. Maybe I can run it by before supper," said Beatrice.

They laughed as Noo-noo glimpsed a squirrel in the enclosed courtyard and took off running after it, barking.

"It's a good thing that I know her squirrel-hunting is completely futile," said Beatrice.

Wyatt said in a teasing voice, "What would you do if she caught one?"

"What would *she* do if she caught one?" asked Beatrice. "She doesn't exactly have a killer instinct. It's all about the chase for her." She took one last bite of her muffin and gave a satisfied sigh. "So, how's it going with this week's sermon?"

"Pretty well. I still want to add another illustration to it. But I don't think I'll be able to work on it more today since I need to run to Lenoir to check on the members who are hospitalized," said Wyatt.

Beatrice called Noo-noo back over and put her leash back on. "That's right. I'd forgotten that you needed to do that today. Or maybe I'd forgotten that today was still going on! It must be the longest day ever. This morning seems as though it were days ago." She paused and added in a deliberately careless voice, "By the way, are there any plans to replace the church secretary?"

Wyatt said, "There was talk about it at the last session meeting, but nothing was decided. Some of the officers were hoping for a volunteer to step in, for budget reasons. Why, is something wrong?"

Beatrice made a face. "I think the officers might have made me the unofficial secretary."

Wyatt frowned. "That wasn't discussed. Besides, there's no way that I'd let that happen. That's not your job."

"Apparently, about a week ago, my cell number was printed in the bulletin as a contact number for information," said Beatrice.

Now it was Wyatt's turn to make a face. "Oh, no."

"I'm afraid so. I've had some calls about activities that I couldn't answer. So that's why I was asking," said Beatrice.

"I'll make sure that your number isn't printed in the bulletin again, although the damage sounds as if it's already been done," said Wyatt with a sigh.

"Maybe I'll only get a few more calls. But it would be great if the church could go ahead and start looking for a replacement for Miss Emily. I know she's retired now and there's no way she's coming back," said Beatrice.

Wyatt said thoughtfully, "Maybe if the session found someone who could work part-time."

"As long as part-time is enough," said Beatrice. "Miss Emily was a full-time worker and I don't think she had much idle time at her desk, either. Anyway, it's just something to think about."

Wyatt leaned over and gave her a quick hug. "For sure. As I said before, that's not your job." Beatrice smiled at him.

They exchanged goodbyes and Beatrice took Noo-noo home and fed her, then picked up the phone and dialed Lois Lee.

"Hi, Lois? This is Beatrice. Piper asked me to get in touch with you about returning the punchbowl she borrowed. I could run it by now, if you wanted."

Lois gave a relaxed laugh. "Well, there's no real hurry to return it. I hardly use a punchbowl every day. In fact, I'm glad that the thing is able to get some real use. It was my mother's and she handed it down to me thinking that I might be some sort of society matron or something. I'm sure she must be disappointed. Dappled Hills isn't exactly 'society.'"

"I know what you mean. How about if I bring it to you tomorrow, then?" asked Beatrice.

Lois said, "How about if *I* run by and pick it up? I probably need to get out of the house some. I've been making lesson plans for the start of school and am practically going cross-eyed over it."

"That sounds great, if it isn't any trouble," said Beatrice. "Just let me know a time so that I can make sure I'm here."

"Is ten o'clock too early?" asked Lois.

"Oh no. I'll have been up for hours," said Beatrice. "See you then."

The rest of the day, Beatrice took it upon herself to try and relax. She'd been so keyed up from the murders that morning that she knew she'd never fall asleep if she didn't make a conscious effort to wind down.

First, she picked up her book. For once, it was a title that *Meadow* had recommended, instead of Ramsay. Ramsay was fond of giving her challenging classic literature or poetry volumes, and with Piper's wedding, Beatrice had known that she needed something a little easier to read. And, preferably, something inspirational. *A Tree Grows in Brooklyn* had fit the bill perfectly.

Wyatt came home with a vase of magnolia blossoms.

Beatrice carefully took them from him and set them down on the dining room table. She inhaled the delicate aroma. "Wyatt, these are amazing!"

He said, "I'd like to claim credit for these, but actually a member of our congregation came by and dropped them by the church—Glenda Goodwell. She picked them from the trees in her yard today and specifically asked me to bring them to you."

Beatrice was slightly taken aback. She had only the faintest memory of Glenda ... and was very much afraid that she was actually confusing her with Emily Thompson. "That's so nice of her. I wonder why."

Wyatt said, "She said that she thought you might enjoy them. And that she wanted to thank you for all you've done at the church lately, despite planning Piper's wedding and being a newlywed, yourself."

Beatrice flushed. "That makes me feel a little guilty. I was just trying to offload a bunch of phone calls by asking that we hire someone."

"But you *have* been doing a lot," said Wyatt. "You visited every adult Sunday school class just to meet people and see what the class was like. You even served food during Youth to meet some of the younger members. And I know how hard you've been trying to remember everyone's name, even though there are lots of members and you might not have the best memory for names."

"*That's* putting it mildly," said Beatrice with a laugh. "Well ... thank you. And thanks to Glenda, too. I'll give her a phone call tomorrow. You've both made me feel a lot better."

Wyatt grinned at her. "And I have another surprise that will make you feel even better than *that*. My hands were too full to bring it in, but when I go back in the car, I'll be bringing in a pan of lasagna from Juliet Winwood. And, I can promise you, her lasagnas are to die for."

Beatrice felt as though she'd somehow won the lottery. "And how did we end up with such a wonderful gift? A gift that will keep me from having to warm up chicken and rice leftovers from several days ago?"

Wyatt said, "Just one of the perks of being a minister. She said that she always cooked several at once and gave them out and that she thought we might want an easy meal after all the busyness of the wedding."

Juliet had been right about that. Beatrice was always a reluctant cook, and any time she had a night off from the kitchen felt like a cause for celebration. She poured them both glasses of red wine, and they talked and laughed and ate and drank and enjoyed their evening together.

Beatrice was startled to find daylight coming through the windows the next time she awakened, plus Noo-noo barking and a noise coming from the front of the cottage. "What's that?" she asked sleepily.

Wyatt was already out of the bed and pulling on his robe. "It sounds like someone at the door," he said, a concerned note in his voice. "Usually I get a phone call if anything's really wrong."

Beatrice groaned and pulled the covers over her head. She had the feeling that she would never get used to the odd hours that a minister worked. He'd been called out of the bed before, but only by phone, as he'd mentioned. Coming by and knocking on the door was something else. Although they *did* get a lot of unannounced visitors—something that Beatrice was trying to adapt to and accept.

But this time there was a two-time murderer running around. Beatrice pulled the covers back off her head and quickly got up, pulling on her own robe. "Be careful, Wyatt. Check to see who's out there, first."

Beatrice was in the living room when Wyatt turned around and gave her a rueful smile. "It's Miss Sissy."

"Oh, for heaven's sake," groused Beatrice. "It's far too early in the morning! And she's been dropping by here all the time.

You'll have to stop being so kind and attentive, Wyatt. You're like a magnet for Miss Sissy."

He was, of course, already unlocking the door. "She had a rough day yesterday," he reminded Beatrice quietly.

"*We* had a rough day yesterday!" said Beatrice.

Still, she managed a smile through somewhat gritted teeth when Miss Sissy, who looked even more discombobulated than she did yesterday, came in. Her hair was nearly completely out of what remained of the bun on her head. The deep wrinkles indicated that Miss Sissy had probably slept in the long floral dress that she was wearing. And she carried a large tote bag that seemed stuffed to the hilt. How she managed to lug the thing over here was a mystery to Beatrice, although Miss Sissy had always had a certain wiry strength.

Wyatt had always been fond of the old woman. "How are you doing, Miss Sissy? Did you have a nice day with Posy at the shop yesterday?"

Miss Sissy made a face and plopped down on their sofa. "Until the shop closed," she spat out. She relented a little, saying gruffly, "Was nice to visit with Maisie. She curled up in my lap for a long time."

Wyatt said, "Can we get you some coffee?"

Miss Sissy made even more of a face, as if the mere mention of coffee had offended her.

"How about breakfast?" asked Beatrice. She sighed, knowing she'd later regret offering food to the bottomless pit. "Have you eaten yet?"

Miss Sissy's eyes brightened ravenously and she shook her head with vigor.

"I'll make it," said Wyatt quickly. "Beatrice, you just have a seat and spend a few minutes trying to wake up. I'll bring coffee to you in a couple of minutes."

Beatrice did sit down, but she was wide awake. She found her irritation at Miss Sissy dwindling as she saw how tired the old woman looked. There were circles under her eyes.

"Did you sleep at all last night?" asked Beatrice.

Miss Sissy thought about this for a moment and then shrugged. "Some. So-so."

Beatrice studied her. She wondered if it would help Miss Sissy more to avoid the subject of the murders or to talk about it. She was about to cautiously attempt a vague reference when Miss Sissy suddenly spoke and took the decision away from her.

"Wickedness! Killing Ophelia!" said the old woman, a fiery look in her eye.

"It certainly was," said Beatrice in a calming voice, "but we're going to find out who was responsible. I know Ophelia was your friend."

Miss Sissy's eyes glistened with tears until she angrily swiped them away. "Find out."

"We will. I've already spoken to a couple of people, trying to get information." The smell of coffee perking came streaming through the kitchen.

"Who?" The old woman leaned in, searching Beatrice's eyes sharply.

Beatrice figured it wouldn't do any harm to tell her. After all, Beatrice wasn't under any confidentiality agreements. "Mae Thigpen, for one."

Miss Sissy snorted at this name. "Wicked."

"Ophelia apparently found her so," said Beatrice with a shrug. "Although I can't quite see what she was getting at. Even Wyatt has wine from time to time and I don't think he has a bit of wickedness in him."

Wyatt, naturally, came in with the coffee at this point and gave Beatrice a bemused smile. She winked at him.

Miss Sissy said, "She is wicked!"

"Well, wicked or not, she doesn't seem to have killed her aunt. At least, she claims she didn't. She says that she was at home. Considering that's how she spends most of her time, that doesn't seem too surprising," said Beatrice as Wyatt walked back into the kitchen to monitor what smelled like eggs scrambling.

"Wasn't! Wasn't at home!" yelled Miss Sissy.

Beatrice took a deep, restorative drink of her coffee. "What on earth do you mean? And how would you know? Wyatt and I picked you up early yesterday and *you* were at home."

"Went to the store early. Saw her there. Mae!" hissed Miss Sissy.

"Are you sure?" pressed Beatrice. "It wasn't the day before? Or another day?"

Now Miss Sissy rolled her eyes as if she was a teenager. "No!"

"Well, then, that's very interesting," said Beatrice, looking thoughtfully at Miss Sissy. "Did you come over to ... well, why did you come over?"

"Wasn't time for the shop to open yet," said Miss Sissy with a shrug.

"The Patchwork Cottage?" asked Beatrice.

The old woman nodded. "Don't want to be alone this morning."

Wyatt came back in, this time bearing two plates fairly heaving with eggs, sausage, biscuits, and bacon. "You don't have to be alone," he said kindly. "That's what friends are for."

Miss Sissy's eyes gleamed at the food and she finally looked like her old self.

Beatrice said, "And remember, we have a guild meeting tomorrow afternoon. Posy will have her part-time worker there while she's at the meeting. You're going, aren't you? Won't that be something else to look forward to?"

"Will there be food?" asked Miss Sissy, her eyes glinting.

"I'm sure. It's at Meadow's house, this time."

Miss Sissy grinned, revealing a gold tooth. Meadow's cooking was as legendary as Miss Sissy's appetite.

After they finished their breakfast, Beatrice groaned. "Now I feel as if I could go back to bed. That was a ton of food!"

"Breakfast is the most important meal of the day, after all," said Wyatt.

"That was more than just breakfast, I think. That was sort of like Thanksgiving dinner," said Beatrice. "But thanks for making it."

Miss Sissy didn't look a bit full and she'd even eaten some of Beatrice's food. And now that she was done eating, she looked fidgety again.

Beatrice had an idea. "Do you know what you could help me do, Miss Sissy? Make Christmas gifts for Piper and Ash."

Miss Sissy nodded. "Quilt?"

"Not a quilt this time, since I made them a quilt for their wedding. I'm making a tree skirt and stockings and it's taking me a bit longer than I'd planned because I've picked it up and put it down so often. I'd thought I'd even make a table runner or dish towels if I had the time, but I'm starting to think that's not going to happen. I have all the fabric, though, right here," said Beatrice.

And that's how the next couple of hours was spent. Miss Sissy took the tree skirt in hand and worked her deft magic as she quilted. Beatrice, who worked on one of the stockings, was delighted to see her finally relax.

Beatrice got so wound up in her work that she totally lost track of the time, which hardly ever happened to her. Wyatt got ready for work and left for the church with a bag lunch and she just muttered a goodbye. Miss Sissy didn't even look up to say goodbye at all, so when the doorbell rang, Beatrice was startled. She looked at Miss Sissy with surprise.

"Visitor," grunted the old woman.

Chapter Eight

Beatrice groaned, looking down at herself. She was still in her robe and slippers and it was ten o'clock in the morning. "Coming!" she said.

She peered out the door and saw Lois Lee there. Beatrice pulled the door open.

"I am so sorry," said Lois, taking in Beatrice's robe. "It *is* too early, isn't it?"

Beatrice said, dryly, "Believe it or not, I've been up since the crack of dawn. I just somehow haven't found the time to get dressed. Please, come on in and I'll pull out the punchbowl."

Lois walked in and Miss Sissy eyed her suspiciously.

"Hi, Miss Sissy," called Lois in a sweet voice.

Miss Sissy growled at her and turned her attention back to her quilting.

"Sorry about that," said Beatrice, returning with the bowl. "Miss Sissy had a hard day yesterday."

"From what I heard, *you* had a hard day yesterday!" said Lois. "How are you doing?"

"Oh, I'm hanging in there," said Beatrice. "Although it was pretty awful."

Lois said in a hushed voice, "Someone told me that you discovered both Pearl *and* Ophelia."

"Well, Wyatt and I arrived at Pearl's house right after Barton had discovered ... her." Beatrice grimaced.

Lois said, "I feel just terrible about it all. To think that I was having such a quiet day while these horribly violent things were going on." She shuddered.

"You were at home?" asked Beatrice delicately. Lois was a good friend of Piper's, but that didn't mean that she wasn't somehow involved. And Violet had mentioned that Ophelia had compared her to Lois.

"That's right. I was still being lazy after Piper's big day. Actually, I was fighting off a bit of a headache," said Lois ruefully. "I celebrated Piper's wedding pretty hard. I've had sort of a rough time lately—my boyfriend and I broke up recently. A friend gave me a ride back home after the reception. Then I spent the day coming up with lesson plans for this upcoming year. I'm teaching fourth grade for the first time and having to come up with all new material."

Beatrice said, "I'm so sorry that you've had a tough time recently. I hate to have to ask this, but I was speaking with someone yesterday that said that Ophelia might have had some sort of disagreement with you?"

Miss Sissy made grouchy grumbling sound effects from the sofa.

Lois frowned. "Disagreement? Over what? I hardly knew Ophelia, although I was sorry to hear about her death."

"That's just the thing—there wasn't really any clarification. Simply that Ophelia had mentioned you in some sort of negative manner," said Beatrice.

"Wickedness!" hissed Miss Sissy softly.

Lois flushed. "This person must be mistaken. I didn't know Ophelia well enough to have any kind of problem with her, or her with me."

Beatrice said in a soothing voice, "They must have been mistaken then. Do you know of anyone who might have been upset with Ophelia? Wanted to do her harm?"

Lois settled down a little and thought. "Well, there's Violet, I suppose." She shifted on her feet.

"Violet?" It had been Violet who'd mentioned Lois and Ophelia.

"That's right. I don't know anything *specifically* about Violet and Ophelia. I only saw Ophelia fussing at Violet downtown recently. And Violet, unfortunately, hasn't been acting like herself lately," said Lois.

"In what way?" asked Beatrice.

"Evillll," commented Miss Sissy from the sofa.

"She just seems rather unstable, that's all. Emotional. I saw her over at the church in tears," said Lois.

"What was Violet crying about?" asked Beatrice, startled. There weren't too many tears at the church. Wyatt always had very upbeat sermons.

"I have no idea. But no one was around her, so I figured that she was simply upset about something. It wasn't as if she was engaged in an argument. I walked over and asked if everything was okay, and she just nodded and then hurried away," said Lois.

"And there's more. Violet has some sort of feud going on with Mona."

Beatrice knew that Mona was another quilter in the Cut-Ups quilting guild along with Violet. "Any ideas what *that* is about?"

"Something to do with quilting I think," said Lois with a shrug.

Miss Sissy exploded. "Poppycock!"

Beatrice had to admit that it was tough to think of how two grown women could be quarreling over quilting.

"How about Pearl?" asked Beatrice, ignoring the old woman. "Have you heard of anyone who might have wanted to do her harm?"

Lois shook her head. "This is what's so baffling to me. Pearl was always so kind to everyone. She helped out at the church. She even volunteered at the school, even though she and Barton didn't have any children. You know that I used to work for Barton, don't you?"

"No, I somehow missed that," said Beatrice. "I thought you'd always been a teacher."

"I worked for him while I was getting my teaching degree." Lois lowered her voice again, giving a hesitant look toward Miss Sissy as though the old woman might gossip later on. "No one is saying that Barton had anything to do with Pearl's death, are they?"

"I'm sure he must be considered a suspect. Spouses always are," said Beatrice.

"Yes. And Pearl could probably be a handful in some ways. She was always very protective of Barton ... always the attentive wife. She'd fuss around him a lot." Lois hesitated. "I don't feel very good about gossiping about the dead."

Miss Sissy snorted from the sofa.

Beatrice quickly interjected, "I know, but you're helping me to form a picture of Pearl and Barton and their marriage. I knew Pearl, of course, but not very well and I haven't lived in Dappled Hills very long."

Lois nodded and slowly continued, "Anyway, I think that Pearl was a little suffocating as a wife. Barton would sit down and she'd bring him an afghan because she was worried he'd catch a cold. She totally monitored his diet and would remind him at parties that he needed to avoid sugar or carbs or whatever."

Beatrice made a face. "That wouldn't be fun to live with—not *all* the time. If you're on a diet, that's one thing. But twenty-four hours a day, seven days a week?" She shook her head.

"That's exactly what it was like all the time. I even heard her at Piper's reception, trying to direct Barton to the vegetable platter." Lois shrugged.

"Do you think that Barton could have murdered his wife simply to get her off of his back?" asked Beatrice.

Lois winced. "No, I really don't. I'm just worried that's what *other people* are going to think. And I'm worried that they're going to talk and spread gossip and that it's going to hurt Barton's run for state office. I can't picture him doing *anything* like that."

Beatrice said, "If Pearl was really protective, I'm surprised that she went along with Barton even running for state office.

That would expose him to a lot of stress and general partisan ill-will."

"I think she was proud of him," said Lois with a shrug. "And it was something that he really wanted to do. I think he wanted to be in politics at that level since he was a child—it was something that he mentioned to me once."

Beatrice asked, "Did you notice that Pearl and Ophelia had an argument at the reception?"

"I sure did. That makes me wonder, come to think of it. We know how nosy Ophelia could be, and how she knew everybody's business. How she made it *her* business to know everyone *else's* business," said Lois slowly.

"What if Pearl was trying to protect Barton again?" asked Beatrice. "Maybe Ophelia found out something that could damage his political run. Perhaps that's why Pearl was trying to offer her money. Maybe she was trying to pay Ophelia off."

Lois said, "That does make sense. Ophelia was very upset about Pearl's offer, too. She didn't want anyone to think that she was the kind of person who could blackmail someone else. Ophelia seemed to take pride in taking the moral highroad. I think Pearl would most definitely want to prevent any negative information about Barton from leaking out. It's something to think about. But it doesn't explain what happened to Pearl."

Beatrice sighed. "It all seems very complex. Well, at least maybe you can shed some light on something for me. Since you used to work with Barton, what did you think of him as a person? Again, I don't really know him really well."

"You mean as a candidate?" asked Lois. "I'm planning on voting for him. I think he'd do a great job; he's always so organized."

"Hmph!" said Miss Sissy.

"I'm sure he is. But I meant who he is as a *person*, not so much as a candidate. You spent some time with him, obviously. What were your impressions of him?" asked Beatrice.

Lois considered this. "He's a good man. That was my impression. I thought he was very capable. Of course, that doesn't mean that he was a great husband, but he could have been. Oh, I don't know. The only reason I brought up Barton is because of the way that Pearl acting around him and because the spouse is always the prime suspect. I don't want anyone to think that Barton is responsible because I'm sure he isn't." She gave a rueful laugh. "I don't think I would make much of a detective. Good luck trying to make heads or tails of these murders." She glanced at her watch. "And now I really must be heading out and back to that lesson planning. Any news from Piper, though?"

"Not a word," said Beatrice with a laugh. "Not that I expected any."

"At least she's missing all this mess with Pearl and Ophelia. That would be sort of a downer for a newlywed, especially since they were both at her wedding!" said Lois, walking toward the door. "Bye, Miss Sissy!"

Miss Sissy glowered at her in response.

Lois waved at Beatrice, "See you later."

"Bye."

Beatrice walked over to Miss Sissy. The old woman had made terrific strides with the tree skirt, as Beatrice had known she would, despite taking the time to listen in on Lois and Beatrice's conversation and making sound effects.

"This is looking beautiful, Miss Sissy," said Beatrice.

"Poppycock," muttered the old woman.

"Poppycock as in your quilting is beautiful? Or poppycock as in what Lois Lee was telling me?" asked Beatrice.

Miss Sissy buttoned her mouth closed. Beatrice sighed. Miss Sissy was never quiet when Beatrice wanted her to be, and when she finally *was* silent, it was when she most wanted her to talk.

"All right, well, I'm going to go get ready for my day finally," said Beatrice. "I'd be horrified if someone else pops over and I'm still in my nightclothes and robe."

Miss Sissy grunted as she leaned over the tree skirt, as if it was all the same to her what Beatrice wore.

Once Beatrice had showered and dressed and made-up her face, she walked back out into the living room. Miss Sissy was gone and Noo-noo sat by the door as if a testament to the fact that the old woman had left.

Beatrice picked up her phone. It was fine that she'd left, but considering Miss Sissy's anxiety lately, she decided it would be best to check on her.

Miss Sissy's phone rang once and then twice. On the third ring, Miss Sissy finally picked up.

"Just making sure everything is all right. You must have found your phone. I didn't realize that you were leaving," said Beatrice pointedly.

"Shop is open. Phone was in the sofa cushions," said Miss Sissy in a careless voice before abruptly hanging up the phone.

Beatrice sighed and then started putting away the tree skirt and the stockings for later.

The rest of the morning was spent on housework and yard-work. With all the people from the congregation dropping by, Beatrice felt that the cottage should be tidier than ever, both inside and out. She was just finishing taking the dishes out of the dishwasher when Wyatt walked into the house for lunch.

He gave her a hug. "How did things go with Miss Sissy?"

"She was back to her annoying self after a while," said Beatrice with a smile. "She decided at one point to ditch me and head off to the Patchwork Cottage, instead. I must not have provided enough entertainment value."

"Usually she has so much fun at our house that she doesn't want to leave. So I guess being boring can be your future strategy," said Wyatt, grinning back at her. He reached down and patted Noo-noo, who had trotted over to see him. "What do you think about taking a walk?"

The little dog alertly tilted her head to one side and then gave an excited jump.

"Are you asking me or Noo-noo?" teased Beatrice.

"Both of you, if you're interested."

"Are you talking about a walk in the neighborhood, or a going-somewhere type of a walk?" asked Beatrice.

"Let's take a walk down that trail we went on a few weeks ago," said Wyatt. "The one with the nice view. I'll make a couple of sandwiches and throw in some drinks and chips."

"If you take your painting and paints, it might be even better," said Beatrice. She'd been trying to encourage Wyatt to continue a painting hobby that he'd had for much of his life. She hadn't known about it for a long time, but now that she did, she tried to get him to paint as much as possible.

"How about if I just bring my sketchpad and pencils this time?" asked Wyatt. "That would be easier than lugging everything with me down the trail. Plus, I don't have much time before I need to head back to the church office."

And so they set out. Noo-noo was grinning in the backseat the whole way to the trail.

"It's funny that more people don't come here. Not that I want a crowd on the trail," said Beatrice.

"I think it's because it doesn't have quite the spectacular view of some of the other ones," said Wyatt with a shrug.

The day was a little cooler than the day before, and there was none of the mugginess in the air. Wyatt parked the car and they set out under a canopy of green leaves down a trail that wound off into the thick woods.

"I hope you weren't planning on getting a ton of exercise. Noo-noo has been in a sniffing-around sort of mood with our walks," said Beatrice.

"I was more just in the mood to get outside after spending the day in my office," said Wyatt.

Their walk was quiet enough and slow-paced enough that they saw deer gazing curiously at them before bounding off, their white tails wagging. A wild turkey startled them and set Noo-noo to barking before it took off. They were nearly to the clearing which had a mountain view and a small waterfall when Noo-noo found something particularly interesting to smell off the trail.

Beatrice was watching her when she spotted something farther out. "What's that out there?"

"Where?" Wyatt squinted into the woods. "Looks like litter of some kind. I'll pick it up. There are some trash receptacles up ahead, I think."

But when he reached the litter, he stopped and turned around. "Beatrice," he said grimly, "I think these are the things stolen from Ophelia's house."

Chapter Nine

Minutes later, they called Ramsay. He parked and hurried up to them, panting a little at the rush, ten minutes later.

"I'm going to have to deputize the two of you, considering how much detective work you've been doing lately," muttered Ramsay. "Where is the stolen property?"

They gestured to the spot in the undergrowth and Ramsay delicately walked closer to have a look.

"Well, they certainly appear to be the items stolen from Ophelia's house," he said with a sigh. "This case is going to be the end of me."

Beatrice said, "So this basically proves that the motive for Ophelia's murder wasn't robbery. But we already really knew that, didn't we? Pearl's death is clearly connected somehow."

"Someone wanted to make it look like a robbery, though. Does that mean that Pearl's death was unplanned?" asked Wyatt, brows drawn together in concern.

"Unless it was the other way around," said Ramsay. He continued staring at the scattered money and jewelry and shook his head.

"The other way around?" asked Beatrice. "You mean, if Pearl was murdered first and *Ophelia's* death was unplanned?"

"The problem is that it could really be either way. Forensics can't say for sure who died first, only that the deaths were in rapid succession and in the same short timeframe. Maybe Pearl was murdered first and Ophelia saw something. Or vice-versa."

Beatrice said slowly, "We know Pearl and Ophelia had a minor altercation at the wedding. Maybe one of them drove to the other's house to apologize or to continue their discussion and saw something they weren't supposed to see."

Ramsay rubbed the side of his face, looking weary. "I don't know. I only know that it's been some kind of day. Did you two hear about Lois Lee?"

Beatrice stood very still. "Lois? What about Lois?"

"She was walking back home a couple of hours ago, taking a shortcut behind the downtown shops ... you know, where that big hill has stairs to the road below? Lois was on the stairs and someone came up and shoved her down them." Ramsay shook his head.

"*What?*" said Beatrice and Wyatt in unison.

"But she was just at my house this morning!" spluttered Beatrice. She realized what a ridiculous thing she'd just said: Lois's presence at her home that morning certainly had no bearing on her being attacked later in the day.

Ramsay gave a helpless shrug. "I don't know what to tell you."

"Lois told me that she was going to stay in and work on lesson plans, though," said Beatrice with a frown. "Is she all right?"

"She'll be fine. She has a bunch of bruises though, and was pretty shaken up by the whole thing as you can imagine. As far as her lesson plans go, she had a whole bunch of papers with her when she fell. And she said that she'd been at the library, which sounds to me like she was probably doing work," said Ramsay.

Wyatt asked, "Did she see who was responsible?"

Ramsay shook his head again, regretfully. "No. I sure wish she had. But the person caught her completely off-guard and it was a pretty long tumble. By the time that she had finished falling and was able to catch her breath, move, and look behind her, there was no one there."

Beatrice said, "It would have been easy for someone to quickly follow her and just as quickly rush back up to where other people were strolling through downtown."

"But who would do such a thing?" asked Wyatt. "Why would someone go after Lois?"

Beatrice said, "Maybe she knew something that the killer was afraid she'd reveal. Lois sure didn't seem to though, when I spoke to her earlier today. She was just making educated guesses about who could be responsible for the crimes. And she didn't act as though she was hiding anything, either."

"Maybe she knows something that she doesn't even realize she knows," said Ramsay. "At any rate, I'm planning on talking to her later today if I can. I sent her along to the hospital in Lenoir, just to have her checked out. You know—make sure that there weren't any internal injuries or anything."

Beatrice said, "I can only imagine what Meadow is going to say about all this. You know how upset she gets when there's wrongdoing of any type in Dappled Hills. She takes great offense by it."

Ramsay groaned. "I know. Meadow is absolutely going to be in orbit. I've already ignored three calls from her and I'm guessing that she knows something is up. Maybe you could talk to her, Beatrice?" he asked hopefully. "You can settle her down sometimes pretty well. I'd love to be able to come home tonight and not have to calm her down. All I'm going to want to do when I get off ... *if* I get off ... is to have a hot meal and read my Faulkner."

Beatrice highly doubted that she had the ability to calm Meadow down, but she gave a reluctant nod. "Of course I'll talk with her. I'll check on her as soon as I get back."

Ramsay said, "Which should be now. Y'all have had a very busy last couple of days. I think you need to take a break."

"That's a good idea," said Wyatt. He turned to Beatrice, "It's about time for Noo-noo to be fed, anyway. Why don't we head back with her? Then maybe you can run by Meadow's house and check in with her."

Ramsay said quickly, "As long as you can find something to talk about besides this crazy case. I mean, fill her in on finding Ophelia's things, of course. But then maybe you can find some unrelated and totally innocuous subject to talk about."

"What about filling her in on Lois?" asked Beatrice.

Ramsay winced, "Yes, but maybe just brush over that a little. Play it down. Then maybe you can segue to something else?"

"We do have a guild meeting coming up tomorrow morning," said Beatrice slowly.

"Perfect!" Ramsay beamed at her. "If y'all are talking about the guild meeting, that'll be sure to distract her from anything else. You know how she gets all caught up in that stuff."

Wyatt and Beatrice made their way with Noo-noo back down the trail and into the car.

Beatrice said, "I know it's early, but I'm thinking about going ahead and making dinner before I go to Meadow's house. We really didn't eat anything for lunch. At least, I'll cook it and you're welcome to eat it whenever you'd like."

"That sounds perfect. But are you sure you wouldn't rather sit down and put your feet up for a while?" asked Wyatt with concern. "You've been going like a house afire for days. Shouldn't you take a few minutes to rest, instead?"

Beatrice gave him a grateful smile. "That's sweet of you, but sometimes when I'm really tired, I get really restless. This is one of those times."

Back at home, Wyatt fed Noo-noo while Beatrice quickly made some spaghetti with frozen meatballs. She didn't feel like being super-creative in the kitchen right then, but at least it would be filling between the pasta and the protein. Besides, Wyatt was far from a picky eater ... and they'd enjoyed that delicious lasagna the night before. If Beatrice waited until after she came back from Meadow's house, she might not have the energy left to cook even a simple meal. And right now, as she'd told Wyatt, she was absolutely spilling over with energy.

After they ate, Beatrice strolled over to Meadow's house. The house was lit up like a Christmas tree, as if Meadow had turned on every light in the place. That just went to prove that the murders were weighing heavily on her mind.

When Beatrice knocked on the door she saw Meadow's face glowering out the front window as if the killer had arrived and was announcing himself. When she saw that it was Beatrice, she relaxed and pulled the door open. As Beatrice walked in, she saw that Meadow was holding a cast iron frying pan.

"Were you really going to use that on me?" asked Beatrice mildly. "A heavy frying pan? I might have to give that a go, myself. It would certainly be an effective tactic to cut down on the number of visitors that Wyatt and I receive."

"You scared the dickens out of me!" scolded Meadow, although she was grinning as she said it. "I was cleaning the kitchen and so deep into my thoughts that I jumped about a mile when you knocked on the door."

"Why didn't you simply release the hounds?" asked Beatrice with a grin. "Boris would be sure to scare intruders absolutely out of their skins."

"Oh, I've put him in the back bedroom with the sound machine on," said Meadow, waving her hands. "He was fixated on barking at a squirrel in the backyard and it was about to drive me batty while I started putting supper together. I decided he needed a little rest time. Ordinarily, Ramsay would be home by now and would throw the ball for him."

"And Ramsay's not home," said Beatrice, seeing a natural segue into the theme of her visit.

"He's certainly not. It's been a very trying day. I haven't been able to get in touch with Ramsay at all. Everything seems to be so scattered and impossible!" Meadow strode back to the kitchen and quickly stirred what smelled like a gravy as Beatrice followed her.

Beatrice paused, picking her words with care. "As a matter of fact, I've seen Ramsay in the last hour or so. He's completely fine, but very busy."

"With two murders, I'd *imagine* he'd be busy, but he's never so busy that he won't return my calls," said Meadow in a huffy voice. She peered at Beatrice through narrowed eyes. "There's more, isn't there? Not—another murder?" She covered her mouth. "I can't stand it!"

"No, no, not a murder. But Lois Lee fell down the stairs on her way home from downtown. On that big hill behind the shops," said Beatrice.

"Well, I certainly hope she's all right, but I can't think what that has to do with Ramsay." Meadow broke off. "Wait. So ... she didn't simply fall? She was pushed?" Meadow's face was horrified.

"Lois was pushed. And she didn't see who was responsible, unfortunately. But Ramsay said that she's doing fine, aside from some bruises and being a bit shaken up. He'd just sent Lois off to the hospital to get checked out, just in case, when Wyatt and I called him," said Beatrice.

"You had to call Ramsay? What now?" demanded Meadow. She clutched at her heart as if anticipating some sort of attack.

"Wyatt and I were taking a hike with Noo-noo and saw a bunch of money and jewelry in a wooded area off the trail. The stash appears to be the items stolen from Ophelia's house," said Beatrice.

"Why on earth would someone take the trouble to rob someone's house, killing them in the process, and then ditch the stolen property?" asked Meadow.

Beatrice said, "Unless the person wanted everyone to *think* that the motive was robbery, instead of whatever the actual motive was."

Meadow nodded slowly. "That does make sense. But it's all so frustrating. When will this all end?"

Beatrice could tell that Meadow was getting more worked up the longer she thought about it. "Let's talk about something else. I don't think I'm totally clued in to what's going on at the guild meeting tomorrow. Could you fill me in?"

Meadow looked startled. "Tomorrow? Oh, for heaven's sake. It's crept up on me with all my worrying about the murders and whatnot. And I'm the hostess, too! I'll have to go to the store. I was thinking about it earlier today, but then I totally forgot about it again."

"The meeting isn't until after lunch—you should have plenty of time to go tomorrow morning. What is it that we're doing tomorrow at the meeting?"

"We'll discuss that show that we're putting on in the fall and give everyone the opportunity to sign up for different roles. Other than that, we'll talk about what we're working on and Posy was going to talk about some new fabrics she has at the store," said Meadow. "It's a pretty basic meeting. Oh, and Posy is bringing Edgenora to the meeting."

Beatrice raised an eyebrow. "The same Edgenora who's a member of the Cut-Ups guild?"

"As if there could be more than one Edgenora in town! Yes, the same one, of course. Posy mentioned that Edgenora wanted more quilts to use as examples or inspiration and so she invited her to come to our meeting since the next Cut-Ups meeting is a while away," said Meadow.

"Maybe she'll have some insight into what's going on with Violet," mused Beatrice.

"Who knows? She's a new member, so maybe she really won't know anything. But it's worth a try."

Meadow absently offered Beatrice the cookie jar, which was full of homemade cookies. Beatrice's phone rang in her pocket and she frowned.

"Don't tell me," said Meadow. "Someone wants to know when Communion is served the next time."

Beatrice said slowly, looking at her phone, "I don't recognize the phone number."

"Then don't answer!"

But Beatrice couldn't resist. After all, maybe it was a doctor's office reminding her of an appointment. Or some other business. "Hello?"

"Beatrice? This is Marjory Beakner. I'm sorry to bother you, but I was wondering if you knew when the men's Bible study meets."

"The *men's* Bible study?" asked Beatrice, somewhat taken aback. And she couldn't for the life of her place Marjory Beakner.

"Yes. I'm just trying to find something to keep Roger busy. He's just retired and he's about to drive me out of my mind here around the house." Marjory gave a snorting laugh.

"One second, let me check." Beatrice pulled the phone away from her ear and fiddled with the apps for a moment while

Meadow rolled her eyes and made all kinds of cryptic motions at Beatrice.

"Marjory? Yes, I've found it. The men's Bible study is on Tuesday nights at 7:30. That's right. No problem." Beatrice put the phone back in her pocket and sighed.

Meadow lifted an eyebrow at her. "No problem? Yes, there *is* a problem, Beatrice. If you keep being helpful then you're going to encourage repeat callers. And why couldn't she look it up on the church website, herself?"

Beatrice shrugged. "I don't know. But it's true that the church website is woefully un-updated. But, of course, that was the church secretary's job. This is just one activity that I know hasn't changed in the last twenty years or so because Wyatt has told me that."

Meadow shook her head. "Something's got to change."

"You're right about that. I think Wyatt is looking into it. And speaking of Wyatt, I should be getting back. He's supposed to be teaching me how to play chess."

Her job there was done since Meadow gave her an absent-minded goodbye and was now totally absorbed in planning for the forgotten meeting the next day.

Chapter Ten

The next morning, Beatrice woke up early and was ready and out walking Noo-noo before Wyatt had even gotten up. She figured ruefully that it must be the shock of being caught by Lois while Beatrice was still in her bathrobe at ten a.m. that made her such an early bird. When she and the corgi got back home, Wyatt had made poached eggs over toast with grits on the side and they ate together while the Weather Channel played, muted, in the background.

Beatrice stared at the crossword puzzle, pushing her reading glasses up farther on her nose and peering closely. She'd made a good start with it at first, but then everything went downhill the last few minutes. And she was pretty sure that 10 down was wrong.

Beatrice glanced over at Wyatt. "Hope the sudoku is going better than the crossword is."

Wyatt grinned at her. "I was just debating whether I wanted to fix my mistakes or if I wanted to scrap it and just start a new puzzle."

"I'd just scrap it. You have that whole big jumbo book of puzzles, after all. If you don't finish that book, then what am I going to get you for your *next* birthday?" asked Beatrice. "You're not very easy to buy for."

Wyatt put his hand across his heart jokingly as if Beatrice had dealt him a major blow. "That's not true. I have lots of interests."

"But you seem to have everything you need. You're very content," said Beatrice, making a face at him. "Which is very frustrating for gift-buyers. I may have to 'accidentally' shrink some of your clothes in the dryer just so I can replace them for Christmas."

Wyatt stood up and walked over to give her a light kiss. "Or I could make a wish list. Just to bypass the sure destruction of my favorite clothes."

"As long as it's a detailed wish list," said Beatrice, smiling up at him. "Don't put 'new shirt' on there, for instance. I want to see 'blue golf shirt' or 'button-down plaid shirt.'"

"It's a plan," said Wyatt, settling back down with his sudoku with a frown.

"Are we an old married couple?" asked Beatrice with one eyebrow raised as she gestured to the Weather Channel and the puzzles. "Because it certainly seems like it."

Wyatt gave her a tender kiss and she felt the magic again. "Or maybe it doesn't," she said with a rueful laugh.

"Unfortunately, I've got to head over to the church for a staff meeting," he said, pushing away the puzzle. "And I'll be bringing up the business about hiring the admin assistant, too," said Wyatt. "Before I go, how about if I give you a hand with the dishes and then the vacuuming?"

"No one will believe you're for real when I tell them," said Beatrice. "But I'll take you up on it. Noo-noo has shed so much lately that I think we could make another corgi out of her fur. If you vacuum, I'll declutter."

Later in the morning after Wyatt had left for church, she was glad that they'd put some time into cleaning. A member of Wyatt's congregation dropped by the house to chat for a few minutes and bring tomatoes. Ordinarily, an impromptu visit would have been something Beatrice would have struggled with, but the tomatoes were absolutely delectable-looking and the grandfatherly man was a treat to talk with.

After lunch, Beatrice set off for Meadow's house again, walking next door a little early so that she could help Meadow set up for the guild meeting and possibly catch up with Ramsay and see if there was any news. Unfortunately, Ramsay's car was missing when she arrived. But then, she should have known that he would make sure to vacate the house before a guild meeting.

Beatrice gave a light tap on Meadow's door. This time, Meadow was too distracted to startle, as she had last night. Instead, she turned and waved for Beatrice to come inside. She appeared to have every pot and pan and mixing bowl she owned out on the counters and stovetop.

Beatrice walked in to breathe in some wonderful baking aromas. "How early did you go to the store, Meadow? Yesterday, you didn't even have anything in the house to eat and now it looks as though you could give even June Bug a run for her money."

Meadow said, "I was there at the crack of dawn, just as soon as they opened. Want some coffee?" She absently gestured in the general direction of a coffee pot.

"Is there any left?" asked Beatrice. "Meadow, did you drink the entire pot?"

"Of course not. Ramsay had a cup."

Beatrice saw that Meadow did seem jittery. She wasn't at all sure that having high-energy Meadow on that much caffeine was a good idea. She was already covered with flour as if she'd had the shakes while she was baking. Beatrice started making another pot of coffee. She'd plan on redirecting Meadow if she tried to have another cup.

Beatrice glanced up sharply at what seemed to be the sound of galloping. Unfortunately, she wasn't fast enough to avoid Boris's love tackle. Boris was a tremendous dog of indeterminate pedigree. Meadow swore that he had some corgi in him but Beatrice was convinced that Meadow was deluded. The only ancestry that was fairly obvious was Great Dane.

"Boris!" gasped Beatrice as the dog licked her face within an inch of his life.

"Boris," fussed Meadow affectionately. "You were supposed to stay in the back during the meeting. It must be all the food smells."

Indeed, something seemed to have possessed the dog. He was bounding around as frisky as a puppy and evading Meadow's halfhearted efforts to corral him.

"Treats," said Beatrice finally. "We'll have to lure him back. Otherwise, he's going to terrify our guest today."

"Edgenora?" said Meadow doubtfully as she glanced around for the elusive treats. "I have my doubts that she's easily terrified somehow."

Finally, the treats were found and Boris was confined to the master bedroom with a sound machine and some chew toys.

Beatrice tried to catch her breath. "That was unexpected exercise," she wheezed. "Are you sure you took him for a walk? You said you were walking him after we met up with Mae and Bizzy at the park."

Meadow shook her head sorrowfully. "The walk didn't work out. I swear, I've just had too much on my mind lately. That's two big things I've forgotten lately—the dog's walk and the guild meeting."

"It's only natural. We've had a lot going on in the last week." She decided to carefully divert the conversation so that the focus wouldn't shift to the murders. A stressed-out Meadow made for a distracted cook. "What's that you're baking?" asked Beatrice as she added some water to the coffeemaker, still planning on making sure Meadow didn't end up with any caffeine.

"Oh, you know. Cookies and brownies. And biscuits because I'm putting together ham biscuits." Meadow opened the oven door and pulled out a cookie sheet of chocolate-chip cookies.

"I can feel the extra pounds already," said Beatrice with a smile. "Seriously, though, Meadow, you know that you don't need to go to that much trouble. It's two o'clock. Everyone should have already had lunch."

"I know, I know. It's just the fact that I was caught off-guard. I'm overcompensating for the fact that I completely forgot about the guild meeting by making it especially fun." Meadow carefully transferred the cookies from the cookie sheet to a cooling rack and then loaded the sheet with more dough.

There was a knock at the door and Meadow started to jog off to answer it as Boris started barking from the back. Beatrice waved her away. "I'll get it, Meadow. I came over to give you a hand, after all."

The guild members came in at the same time, all exclaiming over the delicious aroma in Meadow's home. Posy said, "Everyone, this is Edgenora. She's visiting us from the Cut-Ups guild today."

Everyone called out a greeting. Edgenora was a rather serious-looking woman in her late-fifties with steel-gray hair and a long, lean build. She seemed a little uncomfortable being in the spotlight, so it was just as well that Meadow called out for everyone to fill their plates.

Miss Sissy made a beeline for the food, heaping a plate with it and immediately diving in. June Bug had brought her niece, Katy, with her and the little girl followed Miss Sissy's lead and headed right to the food ... cookies, for her. She sat down next to Miss Sissy who greedily guarded her plate in case the child decided she wanted any cookies off her plate. Georgia walked up to Beatrice while Savannah sat down in a quiet corner nearby and started working on some hand-piecing.

Posy asked Savannah, "Doesn't the food smell delicious? I'm going to have some sweets. Would you like me to bring you a plate?"

Savannah gave her a tight smile and shook her head briskly. "No thank you."

Georgia asked Beatrice, a hint of worry in her voice, "Any information about what's happening with the murders?" Georgia reddened. "Oh, sorry. I really shouldn't have said anything until after the meeting. Especially with a guest here. I've just been so worried. To have something like that happen twice on the same day!"

Beatrice said, "A few things, but we're definitely not close to finding out who was responsible." Posy walked by and Beatrice asked, "Posy, did you happen to see Violet Louise at the church bake sale Sunday morning?"

Posy blinked for a moment as she thought. Then she bobbed her head. "I did, just briefly. There was a lot of coming and going. I couldn't say for sure if she was there for the whole time." Then Katy called her and Posy said, "Sorry, Beatrice."

"Oh, it's fine. Thanks, Posy." Beatrice lowered her voice and turned to Savannah and Georgia, "Do you know anything else about Mae Thigpen? As a neighbor? She's someone who doesn't really offer a lot of information up front. Meadow and I did have the chance to catch her walking her dog, so thanks for that tip. It's just not easy to keep her talking for very long."

Georgia said slowly, "Most of the times she keeps to herself. She's not what I'd call the *friendliest* neighbor in the world. I wasn't sorry to move away. I'd say hi and she'd give a little wave. If we were at the mailbox at the same time or putting our trash out together, she wouldn't ever come over to chat; she'd just give that quick wave and hurried back in."

"I sense there's a '*but*' coming," said Beatrice.

"That's just the thing. She keeps to herself *most* of the time. But she has entertained people at her house in the past. Or, rather, *person*," said Georgia meaningfully. She flushed.

Beatrice waited for her to spit it out. When Georgia hesitated, Beatrice said, "There's someone in particular? Don't worry—this isn't gossip. Any information you have could be really helpful."

Georgia said, "Barton Perry has visited her there pretty regularly. I've seen him leave quite a few times, always in a rush. One time he said something about bringing Mae some of his wife's tomatoes."

Savannah, despite her absorption in her hand piecing, appeared to be listening, too. She snorted. "That's some excuse."

Miss Sissy, who'd been peering at them above her plate of food, suddenly exploded. "Wickedness!"

This startled Katy, who was sitting beside her. Miss Sissy reached out and gave the child a cookie as an apology.

The women lowered their voices. "Maybe he *did* bring tomatoes sometimes. But other times he didn't seem to be carrying anything at all," added Georgia.

Beatrice said thoughtfully, "The fact that Mae does keep to herself would make her the perfect person to have an affair with. She'd be very discreet. And she is an attractive woman."

"But what would that have to do with the fact that Pearl and Ophelia died?" asked Georgia. "How would a possible affair between Mae and Barton play into the equation?"

"Maybe it doesn't really factor in at all," said Beatrice. She was saved from having to respond further to the topic as Meadow called the guild meeting to order. Because, what she was really thinking was that Mae could have wanted to get Pearl out of the way. And then Ophelia, busybody that she was, somehow saw or heard something and Mae had to get rid of her, too ... aunt or no aunt.

The meeting went smoothly. They all snacked far too much on Meadow's delicious biscuits and cookies and drank a lot of homemade lemonade. Posy stood up and gave a little talk about some of the new notions and fabrics that she was carrying at her store before asking everyone to share what project they were currently working on. Edgenora took a notepad and a pencil out of her black patent leather bag and briskly took notes.

After everyone had talked about their quilts, Posy broached shyly, "I wondered if anyone would be interested in participating in a round-robin project? I thought maybe it would be a fun break and spark a little creativity."

Meadow said, "Oh, I would! I'm completely sick of working on my Cathedral Window print. I've been way too distracted to have taken on such a difficult project. I need a break."

Edgenora said curiously, "Cathedral Window? Why did you choose it?"

"I haven't the slightest idea. I must have been out of my mind. I started working on it in the middle of wedding preparations for my son," said Meadow. "Do you remember what possessed me to start on such a hard quilt, Beatrice?"

Beatrice said dryly, "I believe you had some concerns about all the scraps you had on hand."

Meadow snapped her fingers. "Right you are!" She turned to Edgenora. "I have tons of leftover scraps from other projects and I had the bright idea to use up some of them with a Cathedral Window quilt. It's also done entirely by hand—at least, the one I'm working on is. I haven't had the patience. At this rate, I'm going to stop working on it as a quilt project and just make it into a pillowcase or something."

Miss Sissy studied Meadow coolly. "I can help you," she said in her growling voice. "With the quilt."

Meadow blinked at the old woman. Then she said, "That's an absolutely brilliant idea. Maybe you can take it with you to the Patchwork Cottage and it can be a sort of group project for whoever wants to take a crack at it. Maybe Savannah?" she asked in a leading voice.

Beatrice sighed. At this rate, Savannah would be onto them and their underlying motivations to keep her busy in no time. She said, "Yes, that's a good idea, Meadow. Let it be a group project. But I want to hear more about Posy's round-robin."

Posy gave Beatrice an appreciative smile and said, "Although round-robins can be easier projects to include everyone on different levels, I thought since we have so many advanced quilters in our group that we might try something a little more challenging."

Beatrice winced. "I don't think I'm in the advanced quilting category."

"Nonsense!" said Meadow. "Besides, it's important to stretch yourself every now and then. You can't really grow if you never challenge yourself. Of course, my Cathedral Window quilt is the exception that proves the rule. Sometimes we can give ourselves *too much* of a challenge."

"I thought we'd do a medallion print," continued Posy, smiling at the murmur of approval from the group. Beatrice knew these were square quilts with a large design in the center.

Savannah said, smiling "I love those quilts. All the wonderful symmetrical lines."

Edgenora nodded approvingly. "I really like the geometrical designs the best, too. Although I wouldn't be able to work on this group project yet. I need the easier quilt designs."

Savannah said, "If you wanted, I could help you take a crack at the Cathedral Window quilt at the shop sometime."

Meadow quickly interjected, "Savannah is an excellent teacher." She hushed up as Posy started speaking again.

Posy continued, "I thought we could hand-piece and embroider the quilt top. We could have a mariner's compass as the centerpiece and reverse appliquéd flowers around the border, if we wanted. But that's totally up to each quilter. And incorporate some fussy-cuts. I'll send a starter block out with some fabric and then that person will add elements before passing it along to the next person." She smiled at everyone.

Beatrice said cautiously, "Just know that some quilters' work may not be as intricate as others' work."

"That's the fun of it, though! If we were looking for perfection, we'd just have Posy do the whole thing. This is a *group* project and we end up with something completely different," said Meadow.

"Can *I* work on it?" Katy asked June Bug.

"Of course!" June Bug said, beaming at her. "I'll help you."

Details for the round-robin project were hammered out, then the meeting came to a close. Edgenora sat down next to Savannah and seemed to be asking her questions about what she was hand-piecing. Beatrice saw Savannah light up at the attention. She pulled out her phone and showed Edgenora some pictures of her finished quilts while Edgenora made more careful notes in her notebook.

Meadow walked over to Beatrice. "Did you notice? Edgenora and Savannah are hitting it off!"

Posy walked up to join them when she overheard Meadow's statement. "Do you think so?" she asked.

"They do seem to have a lot in common. They're both pretty stern personalities," said Beatrice.

"Savannah is only stern until you really get to know her," said Meadow in her stage whisper. "But I know what you mean. They're serious. And what are the chances of Savannah meeting someone else who was into those geometric designs as much as she is?"

Beatrice said, "I know. They're the only type of quilt that Savannah does, unless we force her to do something different with a group project."

"It's still such a pity that we weren't able to recruit Edgenora into the Village Quilters. Then Savannah would be able to spend more time with her," fretted Meadow.

"Savannah seems to have more than enough free time to be able to meet up with Edgenora even outside the guild meetings," said Beatrice with a shrug. "Her accounting work doesn't keep her tied up all day. And she works from home most of the time."

Posy said hesitantly, "Maybe I should ask Savannah to give Edgenora a hand with her quilting. I could offer to let them work at the Patchwork Cottage. That way Edgenora could meet some other people in town, since she's a newcomer. Who knows, maybe they could even take a stab at the Cathedral Window quilt, since Savannah mentioned it specifically."

Meadow beamed at her. "That's the perfect idea! Thanks, Posy. And you've no clue how glad I am to be done with that quilt. It kept staring at me and making me feel guilty whenever I put my feet up."

Posy hurried off to suggest her plan to the two women. Beatrice's cell phone rang and she stared down at it with irritation as she pulled it from her pocket. Meadow rolled her eyes.

"Hello? The church consignment sale? One second." Beatrice pulled up the church's calendar on her phone and then said, "It's going to be two weeks from Saturday. That's right—two weeks from *this* Saturday. All right." She looked at Meadow. "Don't say it. I already know what you were going to say."

"You're waaaayy too helpful," said Meadow. "But while you're being so helpful and knowledgeable, you *can* answer one church-related question for me."

"If I can," said Beatrice with a sigh. "And if it's on the church calendar."

Meadow leaned in a little closer to Beatrice. "I was trying to keep this meeting on the light side for our visitor, but I've been wondering if you knew when Pearl's funeral was. Or maybe Ophelia's?"

Beatrice said, "Me? Oh, you mean because of Wyatt officiating. Actually, believe it or not, I forgot to ask him about it and it didn't come up in conversation. Let me text him real quick. That's the kind of thing that's definitely *not* on the church calendar."

"That's good. I think most of the women here would want to go to Pearl's funeral, at the very least," said Meadow. "I'll make a quick announcement before everyone heads out."

A few minutes of texting later, Beatrice said, "Wyatt says that Pearl's is tomorrow at ten a.m."

"And Ophelia's?" asked Meadow.

Beatrice shook her head. "No service for Ophelia. She is being cremated and Mae chose not to have a memorial service."

Meadow blinked. "No memorial service? But Ophelia has been a part of Dappled Hills her whole life. It seems like she should at least have some sort of send-off party, even if she could be a difficult person sometimes."

Beatrice shrugged. "I suppose that Mae was the only family Ophelia had and it was up to her."

"She *really* must not have liked her," said Meadow, hands on her hips.

"That was certainly the impression that I got when we were talking to her," said Beatrice dryly. "And I need to speak with her again. I wanted to follow-up with her on some things."

"Another walk in the park with Noo-noo?" asked Meadow brightly. "Or maybe we could bring Boris with us this time."

Beatrice made a face. "No thanks. Especially since your Boris is still overdue for his walk. I'm hoping I'll just run into her downtown. She *does* leave her house, clearly, for things other than taking the dog for walks. Mae must get groceries and go to the drugstore and so forth. I'll keep my eyes peeled for her." Beatrice looked at her watch. "I'd better head on out."

"Want me to pick you up for the funeral tomorrow? I wouldn't think you'd want to ride with Wyatt, would you? He'll be going much earlier than you'd need to. Maybe I could pick you up at 9:30?"

"See you then," said Beatrice.

She walked back home, and on the way realized that there was no coffee in her house. Although there were many things she'd delay going to the store for, coffee was not one of them. She went briefly inside to get her keys and purse and then set off for the store. As she passed the church on the way, she spotted Violet walking out to the parking lot. Beatrice hesitated for a moment and then pulled in, rolling down her window.

Chapter Eleven

"Hi, Violet!" said Beatrice, smiling at her.

"Oh, hi," said Violet with a smile. "Do you have your little dog with you again?"

"Not today, I'm afraid. I'm about to run an errand but saw you here and thought I'd just say hi. You've been working here again?" asked Beatrice.

Violet laughed. "Yes, I have to pay for my expensive quilting hobby somehow. Fortunately, the church always seems to need help."

"It sounds as though the church is lucky to have you," said Beatrice. "And yes, there are always a ton of activities going on at once. I'm sure there's a nursery open for many of them."

Violet said, "How is everything going? Did you hear anything else about Pearl or Ophelia's deaths?" Her face flushed a little as she brought it up. "I figure the minister's wife is bound to know a lot of things that go on around here."

Beatrice said, "Not much, but did you hear about Lois Lee?"

"I did," said Violet. "Poor thing. That was quite a fall she took. I saw her right after it happened. I offered to help her, but she said she was fine."

Beatrice said, "She's fine, but she must have really been shaken up. It's hard to imagine someone pushing her down the stairs like that."

Violet looked at Beatrice steadily. "Yes. It really is." She looked at her watch and said quickly, "I'm sorry, Beatrice, but I have to run. I have another job to get to. Good talking to you."

Beatrice waved to her and drove off.

Bub's Grocery was an ancient grocery store in downtown. It was made of stone, and ivy covered much of the outside. Three old men were apparently permanent fixtures in the rocking chairs outside since Beatrice nearly always saw them there. It was a serviceable store, even if it didn't carry all the things that the stores in Atlanta had. But it wasn't as if Beatrice were trying to make serious cuisine, either. It provided exactly what Beatrice needed.

She walked inside and glanced around the store. Beatrice liked to know when there were a lot of congregation members in there so that she would be prepared with a smile and a name when she was approached. They were always friendly, but it was hard to suddenly have so many people who were trying to make your acquaintance. She felt bad if she stumbled on a name or completely blanked out on one altogether.

Beatrice's eyes narrowed. The store was actually very quiet, but there was one person in there that she wanted to speak to. Mae Thigpen. She was at the back of the store, standing in the dairy section. Beatrice, instead of going straight to the coffee aisle, hurried over to talk with her. She winced a little as she walked. Now she was behaving exactly like the members of the congregation who sometimes descended on her.

"Mae?" asked Beatrice.

Mae turned around and gave her a sharp look. Then her expression turned more resigned. She'd lived in Dappled Hills long enough to know that there was no such thing as privacy here.

She gave Beatrice a crooked half-smile. "Good to see you," she said in a tone that indicated that she was in a tremendous hurry to be on her way.

"Good to see you, too," said Beatrice. She scrambled for a way to extend their conversation before jumping right into questioning her in the middle of the grocery store. "Uh, I wanted to ask you about the plans for your aunt's funeral."

Mae lifted an eyebrow. "Didn't Wyatt tell you? I'm not actually having a funeral for her. She's to be cremated and I don't plan on a memorial service."

Beatrice flushed. "Now that you mention it, I suppose Wyatt did say something to me about it. Well, now that I have you, do you mind if I ask you a couple of questions? There were just a few things that I didn't understand." Beatrice figured that, where Mae was concerned, it was better to simply be direct.

"Sure." Mae folded her arms across her chest and leaned back slightly on the dairy case.

Beatrice took a deep breath. "There was some contradiction in what I thought I heard you say and what I've heard others say. I believe you mentioned that you were at home during the time of Pearl's and Ophelia's deaths."

"If the deaths were the time I thought they were ... yes. In the morning, is what I understood," said Mae. "But it wasn't much of a stretch. I'm *usually* at home." Mae's expression clearly stated that she wished she were back at home right then.

"The odd thing is that I spoke with someone and she was quite certain that she had seen you here at the store during that time," said Beatrice. In fact, Miss Sissy had been more than certain. She had been rather dogmatic about it.

Mae's brow crinkled and she gave Beatrice an appraising look. "If I was at the store, I don't recall it. It's always possible that I dashed out for a missing item, bought it, and then dashed back. Similar to what you're doing."

"Similar to me?" asked Beatrice.

"Exactly. You don't have a cart. You're likely running in for one or two items before leaving," said Mae coolly.

Mae was obviously observant, too. Beatrice said, "That could be. But it's not the same as staying at home. And speaking of being at home, it sounds as if you *do* receive visitors there. It isn't as if you're completely reclusive."

Mae gave her a sharp look again. "I never claimed to be completely reclusive. That's just what the town thinks of someone who works from home and doesn't interact with people a lot."

Beatrice cleared her throat and said softly, although no one was nearby, "I heard that Barton Perry sometimes comes to visit."

Her words seemed to fall like rocks in the quiet of the grocery store. Mae's eyes were cold as she stared at Beatrice and then she gave a harsh laugh. "I shouldn't be surprised. The people in Dappled Hills don't do anything but gossip. Maybe Barton did come over once. Maybe twice. He drops by to bring me things from his garden and whatnot."

Beatrice said, "It sounded as if it were a lot more frequent and a lot less-casual than that."

Mae stared at her, stony-faced. Then Beatrice saw something change in her eyes. Some sort of realization. Mae said slowly, "All right. So what if he did? We've been friends. He and his wife hadn't been close for many years."

"More than friends?" prompted Beatrice.

"*More* than friends. Look, I'll admit it … I've been lonely since my husband's death. When Jeff died, I went through a long period of time when I just felt sort of dead inside. I thought that relationships were over for me. I never expected to enjoy a man's company again, since Jeff and I were so close and I missed him so much. But my relationship with Barton is all over now, although I never asked much of him. He very abruptly dumped me on the phone." Mae rolled her eyes as if it was typical of men to do such a thing.

"Barton broke off your affair before or after Pearl's death?" asked Beatrice.

"Before," said Mae succinctly.

Beatrice said, "Do you think he felt guilty?"

Mae raised her eyebrow again. "Guilty because he killed her?"

"Guilty because he'd been seeing someone behind her back," said Beatrice. "Perhaps he couldn't handle living in the same house with Pearl and having to constantly lie to her."

"If so, that's a stupid reason to break up with someone," said Mae. "After all, he clearly thought he could handle the lying part before he embarked on our relationship. Besides, lying to Pearl isn't a factor anymore and we're still not back together."

"In a town like Dappled Hills, though, if he were seen with you too soon after Pearl's death, tongues would be wagging."

"They wag anyway," muttered Mae, giving Beatrice a dour look.

"But Barton is a politician, running for state office. He needs to make sure that no one is thinking badly of him or, worse, gossiping. Especially now. Pearl will be looked at as sort of a saint, especially after the violent nature of her death. It would be even tougher for Barton to have a public relationship," said Beatrice.

"Which all sounds very reasonable except that Barton and I never *had* a public relationship. Nor did I want one. There was no need for the two of us to suddenly be flitting around at the various Dappled Hills eateries, showing off the fact that we were a couple," said Mae. "No, I think Barton believes that he simply has no time in the day for me now. He's all about community service and serving in the church and being very visible ... finding ways for everyone in town to see him in a positive light," said Mae.

"Maybe he'll increase that community service time now that Pearl is gone," mused Beatrice.

"He might as well," said Mae with a shrug. "He's always felt a sort of void in his life and has looked for ways to fill it. I was one way, once. Now it's work. Soon it will be an elected office on the state level. He'll probably need to jump into more campaigning, too. He really hasn't even done that much. Barton should be traveling around the state and making stump speeches at mom and pop restaurants and that kind of thing."

Beatrice said slowly, "Since you knew Barton so well, do you think it was at all in character for him to have had anything to do with his wife's murder?"

Mae opened her mouth as if to automatically deny this, but then shut it again. When she started talking, her words were measured. "Of course, I wouldn't want to think so. I would never have been with him if I'd thought that he was at all violent. But he does have a terrible temper."

"You've seen his temper?" asked Beatrice.

"On occasion. Never directed at *me* but directed at the world around him. Whenever something doesn't exactly go his way, Barton feels as if the deck is stacked against him. And Pearl could be very frustrating to live with; at least, that's what Barton told me. She babied him beyond belief and was so protective of him. I think it drove him absolutely crazy."

"You believe he might have murdered her then," said Beatrice.

"I think he could have *accidentally* killed her. I don't for a minute believe that there's any way that he created some scheme to murder his wife. But in the heat of the moment, if he'd reached out for her in impulsive anger? It could have happened," said Mae with a slight shrug.

"That explains Pearl, but what about Ophelia?" asked Beatrice. "If Barton murdered his wife, then why would he murder your aunt?"

Mae said, "As far as I could tell, Aunt Ophelia was a very nosy woman. In fact, Barton commented on it once. Apparently, she'd seen him arrive at my house one day when she was trying to drop by for one of her visits. After she'd seen him there, she wouldn't leave me alone. Ophelia kept dropping by to warn me of the dangers of seeing a married man, or calling me on the phone and leaving messages saying that my reputation in Dappled Hills would be ruined if I didn't stop seeing him. Barton called her 'a very dangerous woman.' Maybe she saw something the day Pearl died. Maybe she was planning on blackmailing him or destroying his political career. My aunt didn't really think things through sometimes. She might not have realized what a dangerous game she was playing."

"One more thing," said Beatrice. "Did you hear about the attack on Lois Lee?"

Mae's eyes grew wide. "What?"

"She was pushed down a steep set of stairs. But she's apparently all right," said Beatrice.

"When was this?" asked Mae.

"Yesterday. Early afternoon," said Beatrice.

Mae rolled her eyes. "Before you ask me, I was at home. As usual."

"I thought you always walked Bizzy in the early afternoon," said Beatrice, affecting a confused look.

Mae gave her another cold stare. "If you won't believe me, there's no point in this conversation. Enjoy your shopping." And she strode quickly away with her cart.

Beatrice picked up her coffee and a couple of other items and headed back to her house. When she arrived there, she saw Noo-noo grinning at her from the front window and Miss Sissy standing at her door. When Miss Sissy heard the car engine, she turned and glared at Beatrice.

Beatrice sighed. She wished that there was a pill for patience.

Beatrice got out of the car with her bag of groceries and unlocked the front door. "Hi, Miss Sissy," she said. "I'm surprised to see you. We just saw each other at the guild meeting. Was there something you wanted to tell me?"

Miss Sissy nodded and opened her mouth as if to speak. Then she clamped it shut again. A wily look came into her eyes. "Do you have any chocolate?" she asked.

"I'm sure I do. Chocolate ice cream is in the freezer, I think."

The old woman was already pushing past her into the house.

A few minutes later, Miss Sissy was delving into a bowl of chocolate ice cream topped with chocolate syrup.

Beatrice watched her, shaking her head. "I don't know how you stay as slim as you do. I saw how much food you ate at the guild meeting and now you're following it up with the biggest bowl of ice cream I believe I've ever seen."

Miss Sissy ignored this comment, instead directing her attention to Noo-noo. She threw her a treat from a jar on the table. Noo-noo gobbled it up about as quickly as Miss Sissy was consuming the ice cream.

"Now what's this that you wanted to tell me? Was it something about Pearl?" asked Beatrice.

Miss Sissy shook her head until strands of iron-gray hair escaped from her already-messy bun.

"All right then—Ophelia?" asked Beatrice, trying to remain patient and keep the exasperation from her voice.

Miss Sissy said gruffly, "Violet."

"Violet Louise?" asked Beatrice.

"And Mona." Miss Sissy took another huge bite of ice cream.

"But nothing to do with Ophelia?" asked Beatrice, trying to make some sort of a connection that actually had something to do with the murders.

"Ophelia told me!" said Miss Sissy, shooting her a look.

This was starting to make a little more sense. "So Ophelia saw something. Or heard something. About Violet and Mona ... Mona from the Cut-Ups guild." It was like pulling teeth to get information from Miss Sissy sometimes. And you never knew when she was suddenly going to stop talking.

"That's right!" said Miss Sissy fiercely. She took the last bite of ice cream and then wandered into Beatrice's living room. "Where's the tree skirt?"

Beatrice sighed. But it wasn't as if she couldn't use the help, especially now that she was about to help with a complex round-robin project for Posy. She pulled it out and handed it to the old woman. Maybe quilting would help Miss Sissy to concentrate. She could use some focus.

Miss Sissy ran her hand over the fabric and Beatrice prompted, "Violet and Mona?"

"Violet was lurking," muttered Miss Sissy.

"Lurking?" asked Beatrice. "Somewhere she shouldn't have been? On someone else's property?"

Miss Sissy said, "At Mona's!"

And that was apparently all of the information that Beatrice was going to get from her.

Miss Sissy quilted nonstop without looking up once. Then suddenly she put down the tree skirt and stood up, stretching her bony arms, which gave cracking noises that made Beatrice cringe. The old woman stooped down, gave Noo-noo a pat, and walked toward the front door.

"Leaving?" asked Beatrice pointedly. It would be nice to get advance notice of Miss Sissy's comings and goings, the comings in particular. Miss Sissy grunted an assent and trotted out, slamming the door behind her as if glad to be gone.

As soon as the door shut, the phone rang. Meadow was on the other end. Beatrice was already feeling her energy level drop.

"Are you calling about tomorrow? I thought we were all set with our plans," said Beatrice. "You're picking me up tomorrow morning for the funeral. Was there something else?"

"I'm dropping by Lois's house to bring her a chicken pot pie. As a matter of fact, I was so shaken up by everything going on that I made *three* chicken pot pies. You know that cooking helps me relax," said Meadow with a laugh.

"I do know that, but I never thought you'd need it on a day when you'd already cooked a slew of food for the guild meeting," said Beatrice. "And I'm not sure if I'm up to going out again today. It's been sort of a hectic day."

"It just goes to show what a total and complete mess I am, worrying over Pearl and Ophelia! Beatrice, you have to figure out who the killer is. You know I love Ramsay, but it always seems as if he takes forever when he's investigating," said Meadow. "He's just so deliberate in everything he does. His idea of sleuthing is talking to everyone in town, nodding as he takes notes in his little notebook. At this rate, it will be at least a decade before he figures out who's responsible."

"That's because he's doing things by the book," said Beatrice. "Since he's a police officer. We make faster progress because we're really not limited by any protocol."

"Well by the book is painstakingly slow. Anyway, why don't we go talk to Lois together? She's back at home and she and I *are* friends. She was at Piper's wedding! I'm sure she'd appreciate a chicken pot pie. Plus, if you come along, I'll give you and Wyatt one of the three pies," said Meadow in a persuasive tone.

That was definitely the deciding factor. Beatrice hadn't even considered what might be in her pantry, much less cooked it. Having more of Meadow's delectable Southern cooking today would suit Beatrice just fine, and she was sure Wyatt would love it, too. It would beat the grilled cheese sandwiches that were Beatrice's go-to on the nights she had no idea what to make. She'd had fond daydreams before Piper's wedding that there would be enough leftovers after the reception that she and Wyatt would be set for food for the next week. This, sadly, did not come to pass. The catered food was far too tasty and the number of guests was far too many. It didn't help that many of the guests appeared to have arrived ravenous at the reception.

Beatrice was about to open her mouth to agree with Meadow's plan, when Meadow said, "See you in a sec!" and hung up the phone.

Chapter Twelve

Less than two minutes later, Beatrice heard a merry tap of a car horn outside. At least she'd had the chance to comb her hair before she got there. She was in the process of locking her door behind her when Meadow hollered from the car, "Hold up! Before you lock up and get in the car, put your pie in your fridge."

The pie, Beatrice knew, would be worth it. It would be creamy and the vegetables would have been picked by Meadow herself in her very own garden. She took the pie from Meadow.

"Meadow," she said as she finally climbed into the car, "this is another of those times when I feel badly because you're bringing someone food and I'm not."

"For heaven's sake! Don't feel bad. We're going to tell Lois that this pie is from *both* of us," said Meadow as she backed rather speedily up Beatrice's driveway.

Beatrice held onto the door handle to steady herself. "Lois will likely want to know which half you baked and which half I baked," she remarked dryly.

"Your food is always delicious," said Meadow staunchly. "Now get me caught up to speed. I've cooked myself into a relaxed-enough zone so that I can handle anything. Now tell me the truth, Beatrice. Any more bodies that I don't know about? Hit and runs? Subterfuge? Villainy? Anything that Ramsay might be shielding me from for reasons of his own?" Her shoulders and arms were tense as though she was bracing herself for more bad news.

Beatrice was bracing herself, too, but for different reasons. Meadow was careening down the street at breakneck speed. "Meadow, slow down! We're in no hurry to get there. And no, I haven't heard of anything that dire. Of course, that may be because I spent the afternoon with Miss Sissy. She did inform me, though, that Violet and Mona were having an issue."

"Violet and Mona? Well, they are, but what on earth does that have to do with what's going on with Pearl and Ophelia's murders?" demanded Meadow.

Thankfully, Meadow had slowed down enough for Beatrice to cautiously release her death grip on the door handle. "Miss Sissy said that Ophelia had told her about Violet and Mona's issue. She seemed to think there was some sort of connection. But then, you know Miss Sissy. The connection is probably tenuous at best, or perhaps a complete invention."

Meadow shook her head. "Nope. It's not made-up. They have quite the quilting feud going on. I tell you, I'm just so relieved that we don't have all this drama in the Village Quilters. It seems like the Cut-Ups has all sorts of member problems. Poor Edgenora. She really *did* choose the wrong guild."

"What kind of quilting feud?" asked Beatrice. "I somehow can't picture Violet sniping at Mona. She's so much younger, for one thing."

Meadow raised her eyebrows. "She's younger, but she's sort of sassy."

Beatrice tried and failed to reconcile this with her recollection of Violet at the church. "I just can't see it. Violet was so sweet with Noo-noo and then so into all the church activities. She doesn't seem the sort to be a ... what? Sort of a quilting prima donna? She strikes me as a sort of passive person."

Meadow snapped her fingers, causing her to take one much-needed hand off the wheel. "That's *exactly* what Violet is! Not a passive person, I mean, but a quilting prima donna. She's a relatively new member over at the Cut-Ups, and I think Mona was used to being the one whose quilts everyone fawned over. The guild would travel to quilt shows and Mona would show these complex quilts and win ribbons and get praise. She even taught some classes for Posy at the Patchwork Cottage. Then Violet came in, and she's much younger, and honestly, she's rather gifted."

"Gifted?"

"That's right. Oh, I'm not talking about her IQ or anything like that. Although, it might be quite high, too," said Meadow in a thoughtful voice. "All I know is that she learns things incredibly quickly, at least in terms of quilting. Violet is like a human sponge. She got started quilting with Posy showing her the ropes and then she just took off with it. Violet asked Mona to give her a few lessons, too. But I think Violet must have been just being nice because she was already as good as Mona. She has an eye for color and design and she's willing to experiment. What's more, Violet is fast. Within no time, she was showing her quilts. And not just *showing* them. She was winning ribbons."

Beatrice said, "I'm guessing that didn't make Mona very pleased, even if Violet started out as something like a protégé of hers."

"Oh, *wasn't* she sour? You could tell at first that Mona was trying to be excited about Violet and supportive, but it sure sounded fake to me. Then she started getting worried. Violet was some sort of prodigy!" Meadow slapped the steering wheel emphatically.

Beatrice said, "I'm not altogether sure you can be a prodigy when you're thirtyish. I think you're supposed to be a kid if you're a prodigy."

"Whatever! I'm telling you, she's good. And Mona didn't like it. You should have seen the look on Mona's face at some of those regional shows." Meadow gave Beatrice a sideways look. "Regional shows that *you* should have attended, by the way."

"The guild didn't say that attendance was compulsory," said Beatrice.

"No, but you're very good, Beatrice. You should be entering some of these shows." Meadow steered briefly off the road to avoid a squirrel and skidded back on. It was on a particularly windy part of the mountainous road and Beatrice tightened her grip on the door again.

"I'm not good enough to win any ribbons at a regional show, although sometimes I *do* like going to see everyone else's work. Clearly, I wouldn't have a chance if either Violet or Mona were entering the same contest. But Meadow, I haven't exactly been loaded with extra time lately, have I? First I got married, then Piper," said Beatrice.

"Piper and Ash!" Meadow's eyes grew moist and she removed a hand from the wheel to dab at them. "I can't wait to see them return home from their honeymoon. I miss them both. Maybe we should take them out to lunch or dinner when they come home."

Beatrice was not eager to see more tears from Meadow. Nor to see her take a hand off the steering wheel. "Back to the Violet thing. Maybe Violet *is* very talented and maybe Mona *was* worried. But that didn't seem to be what Miss Sissy was alluding to. She said that Violet was *lurking*."

Meadow wrinkled her nose. "Lurking?"

"Yes. And that doesn't seem to apply to quilting in any way that I can figure," said Beatrice. "Lurking where? Lurking around at Mona's house to ask her for help with her quilts? Help that she apparently didn't even need?"

"Well, I'll have to think about that one," said Meadow. "Hm. Lurking." She brightened and turned to look at Beatrice, turning the wheel in the process before straightening it out again in a hurry and diligently turning her eyes back on the road. "You know, you could ask Mona herself. She works at the garden center."

Beatrice said, "I could probably use a trip to the garden center. I haven't had any real time to spend out in the yard, either."

"You won't get any houseplants, I'm guessing," said Meadow with a snort.

"No. You remember what happened the last time I tried to keep a houseplant alive." Beatrice shuddered. "I can grow things out in the yard, it's just keeping them going inside that's complicated. They'll sit in a corner of my living room for a while and

I'll think everything is fine. Then they start looking stressed and I leap into action, deluging them with water and putting them in sunbeams. Then they look deathly ill and I stop overwatering and put them in the shade. At the very end, I'll usually try a Hail Mary pass and stick them outdoors where they finally give up the ghost altogether. It's a very depressing cycle."

"Well, just stick with what you know. When you focus on your garden, everything works out fine. You even won 'yard of the month' from our neighborhood," said Meadow.

"That was last summer and that was only because I had way too much time on my hands," said Beatrice dryly. "There's no chance of that happening again with weddings galore, trying to figure out what it means to be a pastor's wife, and with bodies cropping up at the rate they are."

Meadow made a face. "I sincerely hope that's the end of the unfortunate deaths. And the family weddings are certainly all finished, unless we find Noo-noo a partner. But good luck with the pastor's wife's education. That does sound tricky to me. Although I haven't heard your phone ring at all," she said, brightening.

As if on cue, Beatrice's phone starting ringing.

Beatrice gave it an exasperated look which she then turned on Meadow. "You're supposed to knock on wood when you say things like that."

"Sorry," said Meadow, although she didn't sound sorry at all. "And just to let you know, I'm going to monitor how helpful you are on the phone call. I want to prove my theory right."

Beatrice sighed and answered. "Yes, this is she. Women's circle meeting? One minute."

Meadow turned to shake her head at her and then quickly swerved back on the road, making Beatrice's heart skip a beat.

"Actually, it's meeting tomorrow morning at ten in the chapel. That's right. You're welcome." Beatrice hung up and looked at Meadow, who was pulling into Lois's driveway.

"It would be much more entertaining if you'd given her the information for the men's Bible study," said Meadow thoughtfully. "What a shock *that* would be to walk into. Then perhaps she'd spread the word that you were quite incompetent at information sharing."

Beatrice shrugged. "Or she'd think that I was a complete idiot. You know I could never do something like that."

"That's because you're too efficient! You wouldn't be able to stand doing something wrong or screwing something up. So you'll be in this position until you prove yourself otherwise," said Meadow sagely.

"Or until the problem is fixed by staffing the church. Which is what I'm pinning my hopes on now," said Beatrice.

They got out of the car and walked up to Lois's front door. She lived in a one-story white house with black shutters. The house and yard were lovingly maintained, despite the challenging yard. It looked as though, with all the overhanging trees, that Lois got very little sun in her yard. She had compensated for this by planting a beautiful shade garden with hostas with yellow and blue tones, golden Japanese forest grass, caladiums, containers of colorful violas and petunias, and red barberry which reinforced Beatrice's desire to go visit Mona and the garden center.

Meadow apparently felt the same way, "Now I feel as if I've been neglecting my yard."

"But you never neglect your garden," pointed out Beatrice. "I'm sure the chicken pot pie will be a testament to that."

Meadow rang the bell and called out, "Lois? It's just Beatrice and Meadow." She said to Beatrice in a stage whisper, "In case she's jittery from the attack."

Beatrice didn't think that too many would-be attackers bothered with ringing the doorbell.

A minute later, Lois answered the door. She sported a few bandages on her face and arms and glanced ruefully at them. "Not much to look at, am I? At least this happened during the summer. Otherwise, I'd have scared the schoolchildren." She stepped aside and gestured for them to come in.

Meadow held out her pie. "A chicken pot pie from *Beatrice* and me," she said, with great emphasis on the 'Beatrice'. "Should I stick this in the fridge for you?"

"That would be wonderful! That's so kind of both of you," said Lois with a grateful smile.

Beatrice followed her into a book-lined living room. Evidence of her work on lesson plans was covering the coffee table in front of a rather-elderly floral sofa. She sat down in a softly padded armchair and Lois sank carefully onto the sofa.

"How are you doing?" asked Beatrice as Meadow walked back in and sat down in an overstuffed loveseat to join them.

"Honestly, I'm doing better than I'd thought," said Lois with a shrug. "A few times last night I woke up with nightmares, but other than that, I've been all right. I think I was very lucky. Actually, I know that I was lucky—Ramsay told me so. And my age was apparently a factor in my ability to walk away from it. At least, that's what the doctor in Lenoir said."

Meadow clucked and frowned furiously again at the idea of someone in Dappled Hills doing such a heinous thing. "And you didn't see who did it? There weren't any clues at all? You didn't even hear them? Someone simply ran up behind you out of the blue and shoved you in the back?"

Lois gave a short laugh. "I didn't see or hear a single thing. Ridiculous, isn't it? I was so caught up in my own thoughts and those darned lesson plans that I didn't even hear anyone coming up behind me."

Beatrice said, "And no one saw anything?"

"You'd think that *someone* would have seen somebody skulking around," said Meadow.

Lois said, "Unfortunately, not. They must not have been skulking too obviously. At any rate, it wasn't very busy in town then, so there weren't too many possible witnesses."

Beatrice asked, "Do you have any idea why someone would have done this?"

Lois said sadly, "That's really what I've been wracking my brain over. I simply don't have any enemies. I've never had a real problem with any of the parents of my students and the students themselves are babies practically, so it's not as if some sort of disaffected student did it because of a bad grade."

Meadow said, "It must have something to do with the murders. What else could be the reason?"

"But why?" asked Lois. "What reason could someone possibly have for wanting to kill me?"

Beatrice said, "Are you sure that there's nothing that you saw the morning of Pearl's and Ophelia's murders? Nothing you heard?"

Lois thought for a moment and then shook her head slowly. "If there's something I know, I don't *know* that I know it. Which is really no help at all." Her brow wrinkled with concern as she tried to work through who might have been behind her attack. "If that was the reason I was shoved, I wish that I could simply let the perpetrator know that I'm totally useless as a witness to any crime because I don't know anything."

Meadow coughed and gave Beatrice a look. Beatrice had the feeling that a change of subject was at hand since Lois's face was clouding up. "How is school going, Lois?"

But Lois seemed reluctant to talk of other things. Especially—as it turned out—school. "You mean last year and the preparation for this year? It's going all right." She hesitated and then said, "To be perfectly honest with you, it's been a lot harder than I'd ever thought it would be. It makes me feel weird to say that because Piper and I were training as teachers at the same time and she's gone on to make teaching look easy. It's just nothing like I'd expected. Piper is a natural, I think. I'm struggling a little more. That's why I'm spending so much time on these lesson plans—I want to make sure that everything goes really smoothly this fall."

Meadow said, "I have to hand it to you—I think it would be so incredibly challenging to be in the classroom. What's the hardest part?"

"What *isn't* the hardest part," said Lois with a wry smile. "I guess classroom management is one of the toughest things.

The kids are just being kids—I'm the one having a tough time with any unruly behavior. I've sat in on Piper's class a couple of times and she simply redirects them with no trouble at all. That's the biggest thing that I struggle with. Then there's figuring out what type of lessons will help the kids master the curriculum the most. Last year I felt as if I was just sinking the whole year, which wasn't a good feeling. That's why my yard looks so great right now—it acted as a way to release stress."

Beatrice said, "I'm sure that teaching school makes your life very different than it was working for Barton."

Lois nodded. "And how!"

"I know you'd said that you planned on voting for Barton and that you thought he was a good man," said Beatrice.

"He is," said Lois.

Beatrice said, "And you'd talked a little about his relationship with Pearl ... that Pearl was protective of him and sort of suffocating."

"She was. Oh, not really in a *bad* way. But I had the impression that it got on his nerves a little bit," said Lois. "Again, I feel terrible about saying anything negative about Pearl, under the circumstances. And, in many ways, she was a great wife for him. She was very organized, for one, and sort of acted as his ad hoc admin assistant. Besides that, she was involved in all kinds of activities in town and made good connections for both of them. Mostly, Pearl was a great asset for Barton."

"I was speaking to someone recently who was saying that Barton had a bad temper and could lose it from time to time," said Beatrice slowly, watching Lois for a reaction.

Lois asked, "You mean a temper when dealing with Pearl? Was someone saying that he might have gotten mad at Pearl and killed her?" Lois blinked at this.

"That was the implication," said Beatrice. "But you look surprised."

"I *am* surprised. I didn't see that temper. I would think that, if someone has a temper, he's at some point going to display some of it outside of the home in moments of stress or frustration or something. But I worked for him for quite a while and I didn't see any sign of it," said Lois.

Meadow said, "Maybe it's the fact that he's a politician? Maybe he's very good at hiding his feelings when he's with other people?"

Lois said, "I really just can't see it. I've even watched him get needled in public by a constituent and he was completely calm. He simply listened to the complaint, nodded, and came up with some possible solutions. That's one reason I'm planning on voting for him." She paused. "In fact, I'm planning on trying to work with him again. I ran into him downtown before Pearl died and told him how school was going when he asked. He told me that, if he wins the election, he has a place for me on his staff as his administrative assistant. I'd imagine that he would especially need one now after poor Pearl's death. That could be the new start that I've been looking for after making what's turning out to be a bad career choice for myself."

Meadow said, reaching out a hand to squeeze Lois's, "I'm sorry about the school. Not everyone is cut out to be a teacher."

Lois laughed, "That's the truth! I wish it had worked out. I gave it my all. Please don't tell anyone about my decision since I haven't told anybody at the school about it. And I'm still dedicated to making this upcoming year work ... for my *own* sake, to at least prove I can do it. I would hate to leave and feel as though I was a complete and utter failure."

"Well, I'm sure whatever you choose it will work out in the end. We're all pulling for you," said Meadow kindly.

"Apparently everyone is! I couldn't believe the number of people who called or came by. I don't even know how they knew about my fall," said Lois. "It's very humbling."

Beatrice said, "You know how it is in a small town ... word travels fast. Although Violet sounded surprised when I told her, that may have been because she didn't realize it wasn't an accidental fall." She was finally able to segue into asking Lois about Violet and Mona in somewhat of a natural way.

Meadow said, "Well, Violet has been out of the loop a little bit, considering that she's been working all the time."

Beatrice said, "Speaking of Violet, Lois, have you heard anything kind of odd about her?"

"Odd in what way?" asked Lois.

"Maybe odd isn't the right word for it. Have you heard anything about Violet having issues with Mona or ... well ... lurking around places?" Beatrice sighed again at Miss Sissy's vague conversations.

"I don't know if I'd say that I've seen Violet *lurking* or even that I knew she was having problems with Mona. But I do know that she hasn't really seemed herself lately. She's been spending a lot of time at the church," said Lois thoughtfully.

"Yes, but she's been working at the nursery there," said Beatrice. "And the church has lots of activities for young parents, so she's been watching the children all during the week."

Lois said, "I'm sure that's true, although I meant that I was seeing her a lot in the sanctuary, during services. It used to be that I rarely saw her worshiping and now I see her there all the time."

Meadow, always quick to defend a fellow quilter said, "Maybe she feels like, since she's already at church anyway while helping with the nursery, she might as well attend a service."

"That could be," said Lois. "Or maybe she has a guilty conscience? She did show up really quickly after my fall." She flushed. "Ignore that. I'm just grasping at straws. I can't imagine Violet being behind any of this—the murders *or* my fall. I think the stress of all this has rattled my nerves."

Beatrice saw the evidence of exhaustion across Lois's features and turned to Meadow. "I think it's time for us to head on out," she said. "Let's let Lois have a little rest."

Meadow said, "Yes, *rest*. Put the lesson plans aside for a while and put your feet up, Lois. It's the quickest way to recover."

They exchanged goodbyes and walked back out to Meadow's car.

Chapter Thirteen

"I think we're on a roll," said Meadow. "We shouldn't go back to the house now, not while we're doing so well investigating. Where else can we go?"

Beatrice considered this. "We could go head to the garden center. I wasn't kidding about needing to do some work in my yard. That 'yard of the month' built up too many expectations for our neighbors. I need to get my yard up to speed."

"Perfect. And I can be there at the garden center to help you lug the stuff," said Meadow.

"Lugging? I'm not planning on getting any *trees*. I only want to brighten up the yard a little bit. Freshen it up some. Maybe plant some flowers," said Beatrice.

"Still, you need my expert gardening advice, if nothing else, even though I haven't spent time in my yard like I should have. But first, we should drive by Mona's house to check and make sure that she's not there," said Meadow.

Meadow drove to the edge of town where cottages dotted a ridge overlooking the Blue Ridge Mountains.

Finally, she pulled off the side of the road so they could study a one-story stone house with a tidy garden.

"I don't see her car in the driveway," said Meadow slowly. "And she doesn't have a garage."

Beatrice squinted at a small structure to the back-right of Mona's house. "What's that?"

"Where?" asked Meadow, squinting herself.

"That building there. It looks like a storage shed of some sort ... what's left of it, anyway," said Beatrice.

Meadow gave a short gasp. "Someone has burned it down."

"Well, not completely down. And we don't know that *someone* did it. Maybe it was struck by lightning or maybe it had some sort of an electrical problem," said Beatrice. "But I think we should find out more about it."

"You don't think that *Violet* could have done something like this?" demanded Meadow.

Beatrice said, "Meadow, we're already suspecting her of murder and of shoving someone down a steep flight of stairs. We might as well add arson into the mix. Don't forget the charge of 'lurking', either."

Meadow narrowed her eyes. "Let's get to the bottom of this." She put the car into drive and lurched off at a fast pace toward the garden center.

Beatrice felt her stomach lurch, as well. "Meadow, again, we don't have to race there. Mona will probably still be at work until the garden center closes. It's about an hour before they lock up."

Meadow drove at a slightly slower pace, but still fast enough for Beatrice to grip the door again, as she stared grimly ahead.

The garden center had apparently been there for ages, long enough to look as if it were an outcropping of the mountain it sat on. Trailing flowers in decorative pots hung from hooks on the porch and the owner had hummingbird feeders mixed in. The pleasing result was of tiny birds and flowers everywhere.

Meadow said, "What was it that you wanted to buy?"

"I'm not sure. Honestly, this place is sort of overwhelming. I didn't realize they had buildings in the back, too," said Beatrice. "I just wanted some flowers to brighten up the yard a little."

"Annual or perennial?" asked a pert voice behind them.

They turned to see a diminutive woman with large glasses and a big smile. "Meadow!" she greeted Meadow. "And ... you're Beatrice, right? I know we've met before, but I'm terrible with names."

Beatrice laughed. "If you're terrible with names, it certainly doesn't show. Yes, I'm Beatrice Coleman."

"I'm Mona," she beamed at them. "And if I can give you any tips on your purchase, just let me know."

Of course, Beatrice *did* want some tips. Mona had been working at the garden center for many years and she was quite knowledgeable. The only problem with getting some real direction and being introduced to so many plants was that Beatrice ended up with a cart full of flowers. She hadn't intended to buy so many, but she couldn't seem to resist. Mona also made sure Beatrice had soil and fertilizer.

Finally, she said, "I probably should check out now. Otherwise, Wyatt and I will be spending the next few days planting. And the poor guy doesn't even have a clue that planting is in his future right now."

Meadow made a dismissive sound. "As if Wyatt would mind anything that you ask him to do! He's so completely devoted."

As they walked to the checkout counter, Beatrice said, "Mona, Meadow and I passed your house on the way over and we hadn't realized you'd had a fire on your property until we saw your shed. That must have been very scary."

Mona turned serious. "It sure was. It was very late at night and I'm so glad that I woke up. Usually I don't wake up in the night like that because I'm a really sound sleeper. If I *hadn't* woken up, I can't imagine how much damage might have happened to the property. Or maybe the fire could have even spread to the house. It's definitely been windy enough lately for that to happen." She shuddered.

Beatrice said, "Do you have any idea how the fire got started?"

Mona's expression turned hard. "I can tell you how I *hope* it started. How I like to *think* that it started. I did have a lot of chemicals stored in the shed for my yard. Most gardeners do, after all. Things to help with fungi on my bushes or problem spots on my lawn. Maybe those chemicals had something to do with it or acted as an accelerant of some kind. Fortunately, I was able to put the fire out myself, but I really hate that I lost so much stuff in that shed. I had collected a lot of yard tools over the years and now I'm having to replace those." She shook her head. "But it could have been so much worse."

Meadow tilted her head to one side at looked quizzically at Mona. "You said that you *hope* it started that way. What's the alternative?"

Mona gave a harsh laugh. "The alternative is that someone set the fire. Maliciously."

After meeting Mona, Beatrice was having a hard time reconciling the tiny, gentle woman with the woman who was supposed to be feuding with Violet. "Who would have done something like that?" she asked.

Mona gave a shrug. "It could have been kids, I suppose. Sometimes teenagers get bored in a town the size of Dappled Hills. There aren't a whole lot of things for teens to do here besides get themselves into trouble. They could have just been out making mischief, not realizing the damage that was going to happen. Or it could have been someone else."

Meadow said, "I've heard through the grapevine that there has been some trouble in the Cut-Ups guild. Is everything okay between you and Violet? And do you think that Violet could have done something like that?" Meadow's horrified features reflected the fact that she, for one, didn't think that a quilter could be responsible for arson.

"I would hate to think that she could," said Mona, looking troubled. "But I can't say that it hasn't been on my mind. The bad feelings between us have gone too far and we need, for the sake of the guild, to become friends again."

Beatrice asked, "What happened between you?"

Mona said, "Oh, you know how it goes between women. It wasn't anything really major; it was mostly just silly stuff that got out of hand. And I know that it was just as much my fault as much as anybody's. Maybe I had a little bit of Queen Bee syndrome. There's not a lot that I'm good at, but I was proud that I was good at quilting. I was even prouder that I was the big prize winner at all of the shows from our guild." Her tone was self-deprecating and she sighed. "Then ... let's face it. A new talent came in."

Beatrice said, "But Violet wasn't that good at first. She couldn't have been."

"No, she wasn't. But she was an extremely quick learner and she was absolutely passionate about quilting. More so than I was, to be honest. Maybe I'd simply gotten complacent after quilting for so long. I wasn't out looking for challenges and didn't put any stock into the fact that I still needed to grow as a quilter. Violet really is an inspiration. Even though she didn't have a lot of time between the part-time jobs, nor a lot of money, she still managed to devote many hours to learning the craft. Violet told us that she would pull quilting all-nighters and then head off to work." Mona shook her head in wonder.

Meadow said sorrowfully, "And to think I missed an opportunity to get her into the Village Quilters."

Mona said, "She became a fantastic quilter. And we all supported her at the Cut-Ups. She'd show up at my house or at another guild member's house and ask questions, lugging her current project with her. Violet would knock on my door all hours of the day or night, single-focused on what she was doing. I don't believe she spared a thought for what we might have going on when she interrupted us. Although sometimes I had the impression that she didn't really need any help at all—she merely needed validation that she was doing well. Even when she was learning, there was an early point when I feel as though her skills far exceeded anyone's in the guild, including mine."

"Her dropping by must have gotten very annoying," said Beatrice, making a face.

Meadow added pointedly, "It must have seemed as though she was *lurking*."

"Most of us didn't even really mind," said Mona. "We were just delighted to have a young member who was so passionate about quilting. We all love introducing new quilters to the craft. But I think, with all our support and encouragement, we created a monster."

Meadow said, "A monster? In what way?"

"Oh, Violet would start pointing out flaws in our own quilts, as if every quilt was supposed to be perfect in every way. Don't get me wrong—perfection is great. But it's not always attainable and that's not always the goal of every quilt. Not every quilt is bound for a show. Violet sort of picked apart everyone's projects," said Mona.

Beatrice said, "That would be very demotivating. And I would imagine that it would really start creating some resentment among the guild members."

"It was and it did. I'm afraid that I started avoiding her a little. Now, looking back on it, I think that finding the flaws in others' quilts was one way that she helped teach herself what *not* to do. Violet was voicing what she was thinking instead of internalizing it. That's me, trying to be understanding now. But at the time, it was very hard to swallow," said Mona.

Meadow said, "Is that when Violet started winning all the shows?"

"That's right. And I feel like I really didn't handle it at all well. Queen Bee syndrome, as I mentioned earlier. I was used to winning and then I *wasn't* winning," said Mona in a self-deprecating voice.

Beatrice said slowly, "But it must have been more than that. How was Violet's attitude about her own winning? Was she a good sport?"

Mona nodded. "You're right. She was a bad winner. Violet would point out the problems, whether in design or execution, of our guild's quilts and explain why hers was better. It wasn't exactly an endearing quality and my back was already up from losing ribbons. I avoided Violet because quilting wasn't fun for me anymore when she was around. The more I avoided her, the more she appeared determined to see me. I think, ultimately, her feelings were hurt. Of course I regret that—I wasn't trying to hurt her. I was simply trying to avoid being so completely annoyed by her presence and tackled it the only way I could think of."

Meadow said, "No one likes a poor sport. But it would have been better if y'all had just *told* her that. Maybe she didn't realize why everyone was trying to avoid her. I would have told her, if she'd been in the Village Quilters."

Beatrice had absolutely no doubt in her mind that that was the case.

"Maybe we should have told her. Maybe I should have sat her down and told her that we were proud of her but that her behavior needed to stop. But we didn't," said Mona with a shrug.

Beatrice said, "How upset *was* Violet? You don't think she'd be upset enough to set fire to your shed, do you? Over something like you avoiding her? That would be rather childish, wouldn't it?"

"It would, but *she* is rather childish, to be honest. The few times that she didn't win, she was just as bad of a sport as she was when she did," said Mona. "And here's the kicker. She was making everyone in the Cut-Ups so miserable that I, as president, called a secret meeting—a meeting where we voted on whether to keep Violet in the guild. We barely had enough votes to keep her in, so we did. But somehow, word got to Violet that I'd proposed removing her from the guild. She was furious. She was yelling at me in the streets when she saw me." Mona shook her head. "So, much as I'd like to think that she wouldn't set fire to my shed, I think it's possible that she did."

A customer walked into the shop and toward Mona, looking as if she had a question for her. Beatrice grabbed her cart and said, "Thanks, Mona. Good talking to you." And Meadow and Beatrice walked back to Meadow's car.

Meadow said as she backed the car up, "Well, what do you think about all that? It just goes to show that it's hard to really know someone."

"You mean Violet? Or Mona?"

"Both!" said Meadow emphatically as she drove away. "I was a little surprised that Mona tried to vote Violet out of the guild, for one. That was such an underhanded thing to have done."

"Yes, but think about it. There was only one person in the guild who was creating a lot of drama for everyone else. More than that, this person was a *new* member. Everyone else had likely been in the guild for a matter of decades. It seems to me that her approach was the most expedient one," said Beatrice. "Remove the person who is creating the stress."

Meadow snorted. "You're always so practical, Beatrice. You're looking at it as a precision cut, something surgical. But there are women's emotions involved ... their feelings. The way

Mona decided to handle it, as president of her guild, involved this sort of political, smoky backroom maneuver. As I said before, it sure would have been a lot better to have a heartfelt one-on-one conversation with Violet. Mona should have simply sat her down and told her quite frankly that people don't *like* having their quilts picked apart in that way. It's hurtful. That maybe it's all right to *think* those types of things, but certainly not to say them unless the quilter is actually looking for critical feedback in order to improve. These quilts can reflect months of work ... you know that."

Beatrice said, "I'm just not convinced that's the better approach."

"Well, maybe Violet wouldn't have burned down Mona's shed, if Mona hadn't been so underhanded in dealing with the whole issue. Obviously, Violet must have been really hurt that there was a secret meeting called with everyone talking about her. If it had been handled privately, between Mona and Violet, maybe it never would have come to this."

"That's true. You do have a point, Meadow. But we don't *know* that Violet was the one that set fire to Mona's shed," said Beatrice. "Although it does sound very likely."

Meadow said, "I'm also surprised by Violet possibly being involved in all this. I've never thought of her as conceited or of having a big ego. Aren't you surprised?"

"Definitely. When I've seen Violet, she's always been sort of shy. It's hard to imagine her lording it over everyone and acting like a quilting expert when she's pretty much brand-new," said Beatrice.

"But that's the thing. She doesn't have to *act* like a quilting expert. She *is* a quilting expert. It simply happened really, really quickly. That doesn't mean that she doesn't know what she's talking about. And everyone else wasn't just annoyed by her manner at the shows—I'm sure they were annoyed by the fact that Violet, who was something of a novice, was winning ribbons," said Meadow. She took a curve on the road rather hard and Beatrice winced.

"Watch the driving, Meadow, or you'll end up with soil all over the back of your van," said Beatrice.

"Oh, right. The flowers," muttered Meadow. "So let's recap things, because I don't know if I can remember all the stuff you've found out so far. We have Violet, as we just mentioned. She might have killed Ophelia, who possibly saw her lurking (using Miss Sissy's word) around Mona's house before the fire. Then she might have murdered Pearl, who could have seen something when Violet was at Ophelia's house."

"Possibly," said Beatrice. "If Pearl stopped by Ophelia's house for some reason that morning. And then we have Barton, who may or may not have had a bad temper, depending on who you're listening to. Pearl may have been driving Barton crazy with her suffocating manner and he killed her in the heat of the moment. Then Ophelia might have seen something and had to be silenced."

"Or else we believe Lois who says that Pearl was a real asset to Barton and that he would never have killed his wife," said Meadow with a sigh. "Moving on to Lois as a potential suspect. Ophelia had something against Lois or something *on* Lois, and Lois might have had to get rid of her. Then Pearl would have been murdered if she could lead the police to Lois. Or, Lois knows something about the killer and that's why she is in danger."

"And then we have Mae. Mae was having an affair with Barton and maybe she thought that, with Pearl out of the way, she and Barton could have a future together," said Beatrice. "Except that Mae says Barton had broken up with her. Maybe she thought that, with Pearl gone, Barton would change his mind."

Meadow said, "Or maybe Mae killed Ophelia first. Since Ophelia apparently had a lot more money than everyone thought. And Ophelia likely left whatever money she had to her niece as her only relative."

"Maybe. Although I don't get the impression that Mae really needs money," said Beatrice. "She seems to be completely content in her life."

"So where do we go from here?" asked Meadow.

Beatrice said, "We'll be at Pearl's service tomorrow and might have the opportunity to follow back up with someone. Violet, maybe? Maybe she'll be attending the funeral."

"Well, Barton will *definitely* be there, but I suppose his wife's funeral service isn't exactly the best time to chat with him," said Meadow.

"No. I think I can easily find a time to talk to him, though. I'll check in with Wyatt and find a time that Barton is likely to be at the church. He's an elder and they have meetings at the church all the time. I'll simply happen to be there at the same time and catch him in the parking lot or something," said Beatrice.

After Beatrice returned home, the rest of the day was spent planting all of the flowers that she'd bought at the garden center. This wasn't the chore she'd expected, but it seemed like a pleasant enough task. She pulled weeds, dug and planted, and even clipped a few of the bushes while she was outside. Maybe it was the fact that it was a completely physical activity that made the work such a nice escape. She'd expected to ask Wyatt to help her after he returned from work, but when he did, she was already wrapping-up.

"What's all this?" he asked, a bemused smile on his face as he stepped out of his car. "The yard looks amazing!"

Beatrice said, "Oh, it's something I've wanted to do for a while. It was such a nice day that I guess I got carried away—with the buying and the planting! I thought I'd leave a little for you to help me with, but I ended up tackling the whole thing."

"I did bring home one thing to plant," said Wyatt.

"You had the same idea?" asked Beatrice. "That's almost spooky."

"Not quite the same idea," said Wyatt, opening up the back door of his sedan and stooping to pick something up from the floor of the car. When he rose, he carried a sapling in his hands.

Beatrice stood up slowly, feeling a little stiff. "You bought a tree!"

Wyatt said, "I thought it would be fun to watch it grow as our marriage grows ... sort of a way to mark the year we were married. It's a cherry tree."

"Those are beautiful in the springtime. And I know just the spot for it," said Beatrice.

"I was hoping you were going to say that," said Wyatt with a laugh. "I didn't plan that part."

"I lost a dogwood a year or so ago and the yard has looked a little bare to me ever since. Right here," she said, pointing to a spot toward the front of the yard.

Wyatt walked in to change clothes and returned with a shovel and some fertilizer and mulch. He hurried back in again and returned with a folding chair "With a tree this size, it won't take long, but why don't you sit down for a while and keep me company? That was a ton of work you did in the yard."

"I was inspired," said Beatrice with a grin. For the next thirty minutes, she watched and chatted with Wyatt as he carefully prepared the site and soil and planted and staked the tree. Then he watered it.

As Wyatt was finishing up, Beatrice's cell phone rang. She sighed for a moment, closing her eyes.

Wyatt frowned. "Is that something church-related again? Are you still getting those?"

"Afraid so," said Beatrice with a groan.

"I'll take it," said Wyatt, holding out his hand. He answered the phone and then said, "Jane? Yes, it's Wyatt Thompson. What can I help you with?" He listened for a moment and then said, "Yes, it's *this* Wednesday night that the youth need to bring soup cans to help with the hunger drive. I'm sorry—did we not update the church calendar? I see. I'm sorry for that. Yes, if Annabelle brings in her cans on Wednesday, we'll have a container to collect them. Thanks."

He hung up and then gave Beatrice a rueful look. "It sounds as though the church calendar isn't getting updated. That's not helping things. I'll sit down with it tonight and see what I can do about making it more of a resource."

Beatrice said, "But that's not your job. And besides, I was hoping we could play a game of chess tonight after supper. You'd mentioned a couple of weeks ago that you used to play and I wanted to see how much I remembered of the game."

Wyatt said, "Maybe we can do both? Think of it this way—if I update the church calendar, you'll have less of a problem with the phone calls. I did speak with the session and they agree that we need to hire someone. When I left them, they were working out the details with whether it needed to be a full-time or part-time position. But as with any change, it's not going to happen overnight. In the meantime, if I spend just thirty or forty minutes on the calendar, it might save you a lot of time." He glanced at his watch. "Speaking of time, how about if I get us started with supper? I think we have some pasta in the freezer. I know you've got to be worn out after all that yardwork. And in the backyard, too! I saw it when I went in to change."

Beatrice gave him a smile. "The good news is that our supper tonight is courtesy of Meadow. We get to enjoy one of her famous chicken pot pies."

And they did. What's more, they ate outside, admiring Beatrice's handiwork.

Chapter Fourteen

The next morning, Beatrice slept a little longer than she'd planned—perhaps because of the planting the day before. She was surprised to find that she was sore from the activity, too. She must have been using some rarely-exercised muscles in the process.

Beatrice was vaguely aware that Wyatt had gotten out of the bed very early. When she walked, a bit bleary-eyed, out into the living room, he was showered and dressed in a suit. He had a couple of papers in front of him and a red pen. He smiled at her when she walked in.

"You're pretty dressed up for the sudoku," said Beatrice. She peered closer. "Actually, that's not even the sudoku. And do I smell fresh baked goods? What on earth is going on this morning?"

"I ran out to June Bug's shop and got us some muffins and pastries," he said. He'd also made coffee and a carafe was on the table along with a creamer and sugar.

"You're spoiling me silly," mumbled Beatrice as she plopped into a chair across from him. "And what on earth are you studying? Oh, wait a minute. I must not have fully woken up yet. This is the morning of Pearl's funeral. Now I remember."

"Barton asked me to give a message at the service." His forehead wrinkled as he studied his papers. "I'm just making sure that I've memorized it. I don't want to have to read it from a piece of paper."

Beatrice said, "Since you've already eaten, why not practice on me?"

While she ate one of June Bug's delicious pecan and maple Danish pastries, Wyatt gave his short sermon. She nodded as she ate and listened. Wyatt had done an excellent job incorporating stories about Pearl and paying tribute to her as well as delivering a pithy message in about a five-minute time period.

"That was very good," said Beatrice after he finished. "I think Barton will really appreciate it. And you certainly know it by heart ... I wouldn't waste any more time trying to memorize it." She paused. "Speaking of Barton, do you know when he might be at the church soon? I mean, not for the funeral, but for a meeting or an activity or something."

Wyatt was still thinking about the service. He answered vaguely, "As a matter of fact, Barton is planning on attending the elders' meeting later this afternoon. Everyone told him that he shouldn't go after such a big day, but he said it would help to distract him to keep busy. And I know the meeting is today because of updating the calendar last night."

"That's at what time?" asked Beatrice innocently.

"Six-thirty. So quite a bit later after the funeral. He said that he'd have plenty of time to put his feet up this afternoon before heading back over to the church," said Wyatt. He glanced at his watch. "I think I'll go ahead and head out."

Beatrice glanced at the clock. "This early?"

"I want to make sure that the funeral director sets up everything the way that Barton wanted. And Barton and I are going to go over a few final plans ... who is giving eulogies and whatnot." Wyatt gathered up his papers and leaned over to give Beatrice a kiss.

Later that morning, Meadow arrived to pick Beatrice up.

"You know that the church is so close that I really don't *need* a ride," said Beatrice as she put a little lipstick on before walking out the door."

Meadow's attire was about as restrained as it could be. She wore a flowing black dress that seemed to be all one piece, but draped in several spots. "Pish! You'd be all hot and sweaty if you walked over and that's no fun. By the way, the flowers we got yesterday look fantastic. You must be super-sore after all that work."

"I was when I woke up, but my muscles are getting better as I'm using them today," said Beatrice.

They got in Meadow's car and headed off to the church. "It's a good thing that we didn't go in separate cars," said Meadow.

Sure enough, there was barely enough room for one more car to park. Fortunately, Wyatt had thought to ask a couple of church deacons to help with the parking and they directed them to a spot.

"We should have come earlier," said Meadow. "We might be standing in the back of the church."

They didn't have to stand, but they were on the very back pew of the church, which was completely filled.

"This looks like an Easter or Christmas Eve service," said Beatrice, assessing the number of people there.

Meadow said, "Well, Pearl was very respected here and a lot of people knew her. I'm not too surprised that it's this crowded at her funeral."

The entire church was covered with flowers. There was a huge arrangement on the altar and flowers at the end of each pew. In fact, if there hadn't been a casket in the front of the sanctuary (covered with a spray of roses), it would have looked more like a wedding ceremony than a funeral service.

Now Beatrice could see why Wyatt took extra time over his message. As she'd told Meadow, the entire service seemed more like a special occasion service than a funeral. There were soloists, a full choir in robes, and a small sermon from Wyatt.

After the service concluded, the family was to go to the graveside for interment, and then meet up with everyone at a reception in the church hall.

Meadow said, "I've never seen so many people in my life. I hope the church ladies provided enough food. I brought in several casseroles, myself, to help supplement. I thought there might be more folks than usual, but I never expected this many."

Beatrice felt herself flush. She should have thought of bringing food. She still hadn't gotten used to this minister's wife gig. "Maybe I should go pick something up and bring it over to the church hall. There should be plenty of time. I'd hate for Pearl's family to arrive at the reception and not have any food left."

"That's a good idea! You could even pick up a couple of containers of fried chicken. I know there are plenty of baking sheets in the church kitchen, and we can just lay it out on those instead of using the cardboard. No one will know it wasn't homemade."

Beatrice reflected glumly that anyone who knew her would know it wasn't homemade.

As she was walking into the parking lot, she spotted Violet climbing into her car. Beatrice smiled at her. "We meet in the church parking lot once more." She paused, narrowing her eyes with concern. "Everything all right, Violet?"

Violet's face was puffy and pink, as if she'd been crying. She hastily scrubbed at her eyes with her sleeve and nodded. "I'm fine. Funerals and weddings always make me cry. And that was a beautiful service for Pearl."

"Are you sure that's all that's wrong?" asked Beatrice.

Violet gave a choked laugh. "No, I guess I'm really not sure. I've been very emotional lately. Well, you'd understand, since you're in a guild. I had something of a falling out with the Cut-Ups. And the guild is pretty much everything to me. It's the whole of my social life, for one."

"A falling out? You're no longer in the Cut-Ups?" asked Beatrice.

"I'm still in there. But I wonder if they wish that I'd just drop out," said Violet. She hung her head and her hair hung limply like a veil around her face, obscuring it.

Beatrice said briskly, always hoping to avoid tears, "Well, I certainly doubt that. If they did, they'd have already voted you out. Besides, aren't you the one who is winning quilt shows right and left? I'm sure they love that one of their guild members is doing so well."

Violet colored and gave a sob. "Oh, Beatrice. Is it okay if I talk to you? You being the minister's wife and everything ... is it sort of like talking to the minister? Private, and all?"

Beatrice considered this. Was Violet about to confess to the murders? She certainly wouldn't be able to keep it quiet. She said cautiously, "I'd definitely try to. But would you rather talk to Wyatt?"

"Oh no, no I couldn't. Not when I've done such a terrible thing. He's such a good person that I would feel even worse," said Violet.

Beatrice noted wryly that Violet had no trouble talking with *her*. She must not have passed the 'good person' test. Before she could reiterate that she would try to keep things under her hat, Violet started talking again.

"Never mind—I need to talk to someone too badly to care if you keep it to yourself or not. I don't really have any friends, you know. I just have people that I work with or quilt with, or whatever," said Violet. She hesitated. "Everybody just gets so irritated with me. I put everything I had into quilting and winning shows. I guess the success that I had went to my head. Maybe I didn't act very nice about winning. I've been a poor sport."

Beatrice said cautiously, "Well, I'm fairly new to quilting, myself, but I've noticed that people can be very sensitive about their work. After all, frequently they've spent months on a project. It's almost like their child—they don't want it criticized."

Violet bobbed her head in agreement. "Yes, that's exactly right. And I don't think I really realized that I was doing that ... that I was being so critical. Maybe I just came across that way. All I knew was that I wanted to improve and get better. Sometimes it helped me see mistakes to avoid when I saw quilts that had issues. Anyway, I have to rebuild some bridges. I've been spending a lot of time at church just trying to feel better. My conscience has been bothering me, you know."

Beatrice frowned. "Your conscience? About being a poor winner?" Or, she wondered, about something far grimmer?

Violet looked away as if trying to find the right words in the woods bordering the church grounds. "Let's just say that I've done something that I shouldn't have done. My anger and my hurt pride took over and I didn't stop them. I acted on my emotions and didn't think things through. I'm working now on improving myself, little by little. Maybe I'll be able to patch things up at the Cut-Ups with specific folks there so that things can go back to the way they were when I first joined. Back then, they were so encouraging and supportive." She made a face. "Ugh. I just realized what I've been saying. *They* were encouraging and supportive of *me*. *I* was the one who was critical and unsupportive." Violet drew her eyebrows down and bent her head again so that her face was obscured.

Beatrice said, "I don't have any doubt that you can make everything better between you and the Cut-Ups. I know those ladies in that guild and I don't think they're the types to harbor grudges."

"I need to especially make up with Mona. Do you know her? She's the president of the Cut-Ups. Unfortunately, I've been pretty ungrateful for all the help that she's given me. Mona is a very talented quilter, and quilting is a huge part of her life ... but the last meeting that I went to, I got the feeling that she really didn't want to even be there. And that was my fault."

The door to the church opened and Beatrice and Violet glimpsed Wyatt walking with Barton Perry and what appeared to be other members of Barton's family as they left for the interment. Violet sighed. "At least I'm not a hypocrite. I don't think that I could stand myself if I was."

"What do you mean? Who's a hypocrite?" asked Beatrice.

"Barton." Violet grimaced. "This probably isn't the right day to be talking about him." She waved her hands in a dismissive gesture. "Just ignore me."

Beatrice said, "It seems to me that he would be even more of a hypocrite on a day like today than on ordinary days."

Violet glanced around to ensure that no one was passing by. She said in a low voice, "I saw them together one day, you know. At the *church*." Her voice was scandalized.

"Who was at the church?" asked Beatrice. "Barton?"

"Barton *and* Mae. The church was deserted and I'd gone to the church kitchen to help make a casserole for a bereaved family. When I stepped out into the hall, I saw them. Barton and Mae were embracing." Violet quivered with indignation.

"This was before Pearl's death, or after it?" asked Beatrice.

"Before. Oh, I was here at the service because of Pearl. She was a really amazing woman and always very kind to me when I ran into her. But I'm no fan of Barton, not after seeing him like that. I'm sure not voting for him when the time comes. If a man can cheat like that when he's been married for so many years, who knows what else he might be capable of? It speaks of his character," said Violet.

"When you saw them," asked Beatrice slowly, "did you get the impression that Barton and Mae cared about each other? That they were in love at all?"

"Barton and Mae? Oh no. Well, Barton didn't love *Mae*, anyway. I'd have said that he loved *Pearl*, even though he was cheating on her. He's a hypocrite, like I said, but I do think he cared for Pearl. And for himself. But not for Mae."

Beatrice asked, "And Mae?"

"Mae was another story. You could tell by the way she looked at Barton that she loved him. She just lit up when she was around him and usually she's a really buttoned-up person. I thought to myself that she was going to end up getting her heart broken. It was very clear that Barton didn't feel the same way about Mae as she did about him," said Violet. She paused and glanced at her watch. "It was good talking to you, Beatrice, but I should run. Thanks so much for listening to me."

Beatrice said with a sigh, "Me, too. I need to pick up some food for the reception."

Twenty minutes later, Beatrice hurried into the church hall with two buckets of fried chicken and a harried look about her.

Meadow rushed up to her with the baking sheets. "There you are! I was beginning to think that you'd had to hunt down the chickens."

Beatrice pushed a stray bit of hair off her face. "Is the family here yet?"

"Not yet. But any minute. And, as you predicted, we're somewhat low on food. Where were you?" Meadow helped Beatrice put the chicken on baking sheets and then carry them over to the buffet line.

They moved away from the line of people at the buffet and Beatrice said quietly, "I spoke with Violet in the parking lot."

Meadow's eyebrows flew up. "Our local pyromaniac? Did you get her to confess?"

"Not in so many words, but I'm positive she must be behind the fire at Mona's shed. Ophelia must have seen her, as we supposed. Violet just referenced feeling really guilty and trying to make amends to people. She's making a change in herself, or trying to," said Beatrice.

Meadow said, "Well, I wish her luck. Changing ourselves is just about the hardest thing out there. But she's young enough that maybe it will be easier for her. And Dappled Hills is way too small to get on people's bad sides. You'd be running into folks who were annoyed with you at the grocery store, gas station, library, post office. It would never stop! You'd have to practically be a recluse to avoid everyone."

Beatrice glanced around. "Speaking of recluses, is Mae here?"

"She's not. Although I don't think that Mae is *that* bad of a recluse. It's not as if she has her food delivered from the grocery store and doesn't venture out into the town or anything. And we see her at church quite a bit, even if she rushes in, sits in the back, and rushes back out again without speaking to anyone," said Meadow.

Beatrice said, "Although maybe the reason church was especially attractive to her is because Barton spends so much time here."

"Is that what Violet thought?" asked Meadow.

"We didn't talk about Mae's churchgoing habits, although Violet did say that she'd happened to come across the two of them embracing at church one day," said Beatrice.

"What? With the whole town around?" Meadow's expression was scandalized.

"No, no. On a day when no one else was here. Except that Violet is here frequently helping out and working and happened to see them," said Beatrice. "She was of the opinion that Mae was more enamored of Barton than he was of her."

"Entirely possible," said Meadow with a sniff. "I sometimes think that Barton is entirely too infatuated with *himself* to be really in love with someone else." Then she craned her neck. "Oh, here he is, now."

As Barton came into the building, he was immediately engulfed by people at the reception.

"I hope someone gets him a plate of food," said Beatrice wryly.

Savannah spotted them across the room and started walking in their direction, a smile on her face.

Meadow said, "Well, would you look at that! Savannah is actually smiling. I can't remember the last time I really saw her smile. I guess at Piper and Ash's wedding, but before that I really can't recall. She must be representing both herself and Georgia at the funeral. Heaven knows that Georgia and Tony are too busy to make it here."

Savannah joined up with them. "A very nice funeral," she said in her measured way. "Pearl would have appreciated the way it all came together."

Beatrice said, "I'm sure she would have. How are *you* doing, Savannah? I didn't really get a chance to speak with you at the guild meeting yesterday."

Savannah said, "Actually, I'm doing pretty well. After the guild meeting, Posy invited Edgenora and me to come by the Patchwork Cottage."

Meadow beamed at her. "Isn't that nice!"

"It was. Edgenora was looking for some quilting tips and Posy asked if I could help her out since Posy is so busy with the shop and everything." Savannah flushed a bit with pride at being asked. She added in a hushed voice, "Edgenora bought up half the shop! She can't seem to resist fabrics or something. Anyway, I helped her for a while and Posy brought in some snacks from June Bug's bakery, even though we'd been stuffed at your house already, Meadow. But it was still so good. After I leave here I'm dropping by Edgenora's house to help her out some more. She has something to do at the church tonight, but I figured we could work on her quilt before then."

Beatrice said, "That's great, Savannah. Is Edgenora settling into Dappled Hills all right?"

Savannah considered this in her serious way. "Actually, I don't think she has. Not so far, anyway. She had less time when she lived up north, apparently. She worked as a secretary and had a lot of friends. But then Edgenora got sick of the snow and had spent time in Dappled Hills when she was a child because her mother had family here. It was kind of a whim to move down and I think she's had a tough time getting used to it. But things are looking up, she said." She looked at her watch. "I should say a few words to Barton and then head on out. Good seeing you two."

As Savannah briskly walked away, Meadow said to Beatrice, "She was just as peppy as it's possible for Savannah to be! You know, she's never really had anyone to be as close friends to her as her sister was. Maybe this will be the best thing that could have happened. Okay, back to what we were talking about earlier. Are you going to try to speak with Barton now? Because it doesn't look as though he's going to be freed up anytime soon."

"Well, I'm going to speak with Barton, but just in my role as the minister's wife expressing condolences. I'm going to come back to the church later this evening to talk with him," said Beatrice. "And after I manage to speak with him here, maybe you and I could head on home. I think Wyatt may be here for a while."

Chapter Fifteen

Later in the afternoon, back at home, Beatrice looked at her clock and groaned. It was time for her to go back to the church if she planned on being able to 'casually' run into Barton. But it had taken a long time for the crowd around Barton to ease up at Pearl's reception and Beatrice had been there a lot longer than she'd planned. She combed her hair and freshened her makeup, and then set back out again as Wyatt dozed in an armchair with an equally-sleepy Noo-noo on the floor beside him.

As she was walking into the church, she heard a voice from behind her. "Beatrice? It's Beatrice, isn't it?"

Beatrice turned to see Edgenora behind her. She smiled and said, "It sure is. You're good with names, I see. There were quite a few of us at the guild meeting, too. I'm impressed."

Edgenora said, "I had to be in my previous job. I was an administrative assistant at a large business. Now I guess it's second nature."

Beatrice said, "How are you settling in here in Dappled Hills? I'm something of a newcomer still, myself. Actually, Dappled Hills is the type of town where, if your great-great- grandparents didn't live here, you're considered a newcomer. I moved here from Atlanta and I was surprised at what an adjustment it was."

Edgenora's stiff demeanor softened a little. "You're right. It's been a challenge. But then I decided that I wasn't doing a very good job meeting people either. I was hardly going to meet anyone staying inside or gardening in the backyard. I realized I needed to get away from the house more since people were not exactly knocking on my door to meet me. I joined a quilt guild and picked up a Bible study at the church and I feel as though I'm starting to make friends now. Savannah has been especially nice and it seems as though we have a lot in common. But I'm still ... struggling, I suppose ... to fill the hours."

"Fill the hours?" asked Beatrice.

Edgenora said, "When I was working, I had a very set routine. I'm afraid I've discovered that I'm a little lost when I don't have a place I need to go every day."

"I know what you mean. I'd always thought that retirement would be this amazing thing and I looked forward to it for a couple of decades. But when it came right down to it, I found out that I get really restless if I don't have anything to do," said Beatrice.

Edgenora chuckled. "I'm glad to hear that someone understands. Most people look at me like I'm crazy when I say that retirement has been tough."

Beatrice said slowly as a brainwave hit her, "You certainly don't seem as if you *need* a job, but would you possibly be interested in one? Just in terms of filling the hours, as you said? And maybe, meeting people, too? It would sure help provide some structure and routine in your day, since that's been missing."

"What sort of a job?" asked Edgenora cautiously.

"A part-time one. You mentioned that you'd been an administrative assistant for a big company. If you were organized enough to take that on, I'm sure you could easily handle a church administrative assistant job. That is, if you were interested. The church lost its admin a couple of years ago. Even though it's not a very large church, the congregation is extremely active and there are lots of activities every day. I've been getting text messages and emails and phone calls on times and days of different programs and trying to field them," said Beatrice.

"That wasn't your job, surely?" asked Edgenora, looking taken aback.

"Not technically, but as the minister's wife, I felt a responsibility for helping church members connect with their events. I'd *love* to be able to tell them to call the church office, instead." Beatrice hesitated. "But only, of course, if it's something that sounds interesting to you."

Edgenora smiled at her. "It sounds perfect. And you're right—I don't really *need* a job, I just like keeping busy. And, maybe, feeling *useful*. Needed."

"I can promise you that you're needed," said Beatrice fervently. "How about if I talk with Wyatt about it when I get home and the two of you can schedule a meeting to get it all set up ... expectations and hours and whatnot."

A minute later, a beaming Edgenora was hurrying off to her Bible study and a beaming Beatrice was walking into the church.

Wyatt had told her earlier that the elders were meeting in the church parlor. This suited Beatrice fine since the church library was in the room next door. This way, she could read for a while and keep an ear out for when the meeting drew to a close. She picked out a book from the numerous volumes, sank into a comfortable chair in the library, and willed herself not to fall asleep. But it had been a long week.

At some point later, there was a light cough and a hand gently shook her shoulder. "Beatrice?"

It was Barton. Beatrice woke up fully with a start. "Oh! Hi, Barton."

He grinned at her. "Hi, yourself. I was just turning out the lights in the church for the night and happened to see a light on in the library. It's a good thing I did, too. Otherwise, you might have ended up spending the night in the church."

"Wyatt would have looked for me eventually," said Beatrice with a laugh. "But it might have taken a while. He's used to my wandering around. And this is a nice quiet place to read." She sobered a little. "Sorry again about Pearl. I know this has been a long day for you. I'd think that you must be just as tired as I am."

Barton nodded. "It's true. I think once I actually *stop* today, I'm going to be really exhausted. But I wanted to make the meeting tonight. Somehow, church has a calming effect on me. It was a good way to end a tough day."

"Has Ramsay made any progress in the case? In finding out what happened to Pearl?" asked Beatrice.

Barton said, "Not that he's made me aware of." He shook his head. "I'm still trying to get over the shock that she's actually gone."

Beatrice hesitated and then said, "I hate to bring this up, Barton, especially today, but I feel as if I have to. I was speaking with ... someone ... and this person said that you and Mae were, well, an item. Is this true?"

Barton flushed and looked away. Then he returned his gaze to meet Beatrice and she saw the exhaustion mixed with a tinge of anger in his eyes. She remembered that Barton had been reputed to have a temper and that she was alone, at night, here in the church.

But Barton seemed to force himself to calm down. He gave a short laugh. "Small towns and gossip, right? Everyone seems to know everything about everybody in Dappled Hills."

Beatrice asked softly, "But is it true? Sometimes when there's smoke, there's fire."

"It *used* to be true," said Barton. He looked at the floor again as if the library rug were fascinating. "And I'll never get over the guilt that I feel about that. About betraying my poor Pearl. I'm not perfect ... far from it. I've made lots of mistakes and now I'm trying to make up for lost time. I'm trying now to become a better person. I want to serve the greater good. I'm working on self-improvement."

This was starting to sound a lot like Violet. "And Mae? Does she feel the same way?"

Barton said, "I can count on you to be discreet?"

Beatrice nodded.

Barton blew out a breath that it sounded like he'd been holding the entire day. "I know you're not a blabbermouth. It's just with the campaign and everything, sometimes I feel as though I can't trust anybody. But I sure could use somebody to talk to. To be honest, I'm not really sure what Mae feels right now. I saw her on my way to church yesterday and she looked so

... despondent. I worry about her. I didn't think that she cared for me that way, not really. I thought our relationship was just a diversion for her. She'd had a hard time after the death of her husband and it sounded as if she'd cared about him a lot. I thought I was some dalliance, a stepping-stone back into the world of relationships. But it wasn't like that at all. When I told her that I was ending things, she took it very seriously. She seemed completely crushed. I almost asked Ramsay to run by and do a welfare check on her, but that seemed like such a conceited thing for me to say—'Oh, could you check on Mae? She's absolutely crazy about me.' She acted as if I'd broken her heart, but I figured she knew the score before we even got started. I was married—that wasn't exactly a secret."

Beatrice asked, "Did you ever give Mae reason to hope that you would leave Pearl and marry you?"

Barton looked shocked. "Certainly not. If she thought that was in the cards, it was her own imagination at work. I never said anything to make her think that she and I had any sort of an official future together. How could I? Regardless of what it looked like, I loved my wife. I never wanted to do anything to hurt her or to bring any sort of disgrace on our family."

"And now? Are you in touch with Mae now? Or is it really over?" asked Beatrice.

Barton said, "I'm not in touch with her. I cut off all contact, and I haven't responded to any text or phone messages from Mae. As I mentioned, I'm trying to work on myself for personal improvement, and I want to work on my campaign. I've even changed my philosophy on the election. If I win, that's great, and I'll plan on using my office to serve the greater good. But it's no longer about me, it's about the people. I don't have the time for anything else. "

Beatrice said, "Just one other thing. I don't know if you've heard, but Lois Lee took a terrible fall."

Barton put on his 'concerned elected official' face. "I'm sorry to hear that. No, I didn't hear anything about a fall. I've just been so busy lately that I supposed I haven't been available to hear the local gossip. Is she going to be okay?"

"Yes, she's fine. But it wasn't an accident—she was pushed. " She watched Barton's face change and a cautious wall come up.

"How awful. Of course, I don't know anything about that or where it took place, but I can say with certainty that the only places I've been are home and the church since Pearl died." He forced a short laugh. "Literally. It's a good thing that everyone has been bringing food over, because I haven't even made it to the store," he said. He held his body stiffly, defensively.

Beatrice nodded. "I can totally understand that. It's bound to be that way for a while, too, until things reach a new normal. At least, that's how it was when I lost my first husband, many years ago. What must be so frustrating for you is the manner of Pearl's death. That you're having to go through this grieving process when it wasn't even a natural death or a death that made any kind of sense at all. I know the last time I asked you, you couldn't think of anyone, but now that a little time has passed, do you have any ideas who might have been responsible for Pearl's death?"

Barton shook his head. "I don't." But he didn't look at Beatrice when he said it, and he moved restlessly as if eager to be on his way.

It felt to Beatrice as if Barton didn't want to implicate someone, but definitely had his suspicions.

"And now, I think I really should be getting back. May I walk you to your car?" asked Barton, chivalrously.

"Actually, I walked over from my house," said Beatrice.

"Then let me drop you off at home. I insist," said Barton. "After all, somewhere in this town, is a double-murderer. And it's now the end of the day."

Minutes later, he'd dropped Beatrice back home. She walked inside to find Wyatt reading, and curled up with Noo-noo on the sofa. Noo-noo grinned at her as she walked into the living room.

"I do believe Wyatt is spoiling you, Noo-noo," said Beatrice with a smile.

Wyatt stretched and smiled back at her. "Possibly."

"Oh, I can't believe I forgot to mention it to you before now!" said Beatrice. "I found us the perfect lead for the church secretary position. Her name is Edgenora and she's new in town. She was an admin assistant for a corporation up north for years and is at loose ends and looking for things to do."

"She sounds perfect," said Wyatt with a smile. Then he hesitated. "But if she's used to such a good position up north, will she be interested in something at the church? And will the church be able to afford her?"

"Edgenora indicated that it would mostly be needed to provide some structure to her day and to help her be more involved and to meet more people. She doesn't seem to need the money as much and said she'd be happy to work on a part-time basis," said Beatrice.

"I'll give her a call the first thing tomorrow," said Wyatt. "She sounds like the perfect candidate. And how did everything go at the church tonight?"

Beatrice thought about her answer. "It was a little disturbing, actually."

"Disturbing? How?"

"I guess you know that the reason I wanted to go to the church was to have the opportunity to talk to Barton for a few minutes. I managed to ask him about his affair," said Beatrice. "Which was, of course, a bit of a delicate subject. He was fairly straightforward about it, though. Barton said that he was focusing on self-improvement. But he mentioned being worried about Mae."

"In what way?" asked Wyatt.

"Well, he said that Mae had taken their relationship a lot more seriously than he had. He'd seemed to think that they were simply having an affair and he intimated that she'd thought it was a real relationship. He said that she was 'despondent.' Barton even mentioned that he'd thought about having Ramsay do a welfare visit." Beatrice sighed.

"That's worrying you," said Wyatt, reaching out for her hand.

"It is," admitted Beatrice. "Maybe it's the fact that you and I have come across two bodies in the last week, but I have no desire to come across a third. Besides, since Barton told me about Mae, I'd feel almost responsible if something happened to her and I hadn't even checked in on her."

Wyatt said, "Do you want me to run by there with you?"

"On what sort of excuse?" asked Beatrice with a shrug. "I only just saw her in the grocery store. I'm sure she probably feels as though I'm harassing her at this point."

"We don't have to make an excuse. We only have to tell her the truth—that we were concerned about her and wanted to check in," said Wyatt. He added wryly, "I *am* a minister, after all. Checking on my congregation is part of the job."

Beatrice nodded, relieved. "Honestly, that would be great. When he said that, I just had this really sinking feeling, almost like an intuition. At least I'd be able to fall asleep tonight, knowing that she's all right."

"Then let's run by there." Wyatt glanced at his watch. "Do you want to drop by June Bug's shop on the way? I think we can hit it before she closes up for the day. Maybe we can bring Mae some banana bread or something."

"Good idea. That might at least get me through the door," said Beatrice with a short laugh. "I have the feeling that I'm not Mae's favorite person right now."

"At least you're not in her bad books as much as it sounds like Barton is," said Wyatt.

Chapter Sixteen

They got into the car and drove to June Bug's for the bread. A few minutes later, they were in front of Mae's house, the setting sun casting a pinkish hue on the yard. But they weren't the only ones. Ramsay's police cruiser was in the driveway and he was getting out of the car.

Ramsay raised his eyebrows as they walked up. "Evening, folks. Everything okay?"

Wyatt said quietly, "That's what we're here to find out. Beatrice was a little worried about Mae after something that Barton had said."

Beatrice asked, "Why are you here, Ramsay?"

"I'd imagine because I've heard the same rumors that you have," said Ramsay with a small smile. "That's what small towns are all about. This was the first chance I've had to talk with Mae."

Wyatt turned to Beatrice, "Should we just let Ramsay check on her? We could bring Mae the banana bread another time ... or eat it ourselves."

Before Beatrice could answer, Ramsay was already heading up to the front door and ringing the bell. They could hear her little dog, Bizzy, explode into barking. A minute later, they could see Mae peering out the window next to her door. Her face was grim as she spotted Ramsay.

Mae held up her finger and said, "Just a moment. I'll put Bizzy up first. She gets too excited when I have company." She left the window.

Ramsay grunted. "I can't for the life of me imagine what kind of trouble an excited Bizzy could cause. That's a tiny little dog."

"Well, I guess she'd be loud, anyway," said Beatrice.

She and Wyatt turned to leave and Ramsay said with a shrug, "You might as well just stay. You've got the bread and everything. Mae would tell you if she didn't want you here."

Wyatt looked uneasily at Beatrice but at that moment the door opened and Mae woodenly motioned them in.

They walked into her living room and hesitantly took seats, since Mae didn't invite them to sit down. Mae sank down into an armchair and propped her head on her hand.

Ramsay opened his mouth to say something and then shut it again as if not entirely sure what direction to go in.

Beatrice said in an apologetic tone, "Wyatt and I wanted to check on you, Mae. We happened to run into Ramsay in your driveway. I spoke with Barton this evening at the church."

"Of course you did," said Mae in a rather bitter voice.

Beatrice continued, "He told me that he was worried about you. He wondered if someone should stop by and check on you."

Mae snorted. "That's rich. That must be the first time he's ever worried about me. I decided that he really didn't care for anybody but himself."

"He did sound concerned," said Beatrice. "And honestly, after speaking with him, *I* became concerned. I talked Wyatt into coming by here to make sure that you were all right. I understand that your relationship didn't go exactly the way that you thought it would."

Mae shook her head, giving a short laugh. "My relationship? No, it didn't. Actually, according to Barton, we didn't even *have* a relationship. It was all in my head, apparently. I was the one who thought that we had a future together. I believe that he was going to leave his wife and marry me. Isn't that funny? Now that I think about it, I really do want to laugh. Me as a political wife!"

Her words slurred just the faintest bit and Beatrice wondered if maybe she had been drinking.

Mae turned to look at Ramsay. "I know why you're here. You're here because of Pearl."

Ramsay's eyebrows drew down in a thicket over his eyes. "Well, naturally. I'm trying to figure out what happened to her and who's responsible. Not just for Pearl, but for your aunt, too. It's my job."

But Beatrice was studying Mae more closely. "You think Ramsay is here to arrest you, don't you? For Pearl's death."

Ramsay and Wyatt stared at Beatrice with wide eyes. But Mae just looked levelly back at her.

"That's because you're responsible for Pearl's death," said Beatrice, drawing a deep breath. "You wanted to build a future with Barton, but Pearl stood in the way of that. At first, you thought that Barton was going to leave her. Maybe he even hinted that he was planning to, just to ease your mind about the affair."

"Naturally he did," agreed Mae, nodding in that somewhat intoxicated way. She slumped farther into the padded depths of the soft armchair. "He said that they were good partners in a business sense, but that they'd stopped feeling love in a romantic sense for a long time. He made it sound as though he wouldn't hurt Pearl in any way by having an affair."

"But then you started pressing him, didn't you?" asked Beatrice. "You weren't content to leave things the way they were. Although *Barton* may have been content to leave them that way. It worked out well for him because he never planned on leaving Pearl. So you felt as if you had to do something. If you got Pearl out of the way, then Barton would marry you."

Mae now was listening to Beatrice avidly, nodding along as she spoke.

Beatrice continued, "You were out the morning of the murders. Maybe when you were out running your errand you even heard about the spat that Pearl and your Aunt Ophelia had at the wedding. It's a small town and news travels fast. You never cared for Ophelia—in fact, she drove you crazy by popping by your house for unwanted visits and giving unsolicited advice. You decided that that morning would be the perfect time to get Pearl out of the way once and for all. Maybe Ophelia would be blamed since half the town had seen them argue."

Mae tilted her head to one side as if listening to a story. "Go on."

Beatrice said, "And maybe your intention at first was never to harm Pearl, at least not physically. Maybe your intention was simply to fill her in on the fact that her husband was having an affair with you. You thought that Pearl's pride wouldn't allow her to remain married to a man who was cheating on her. If you told her about your affair with Barton, maybe she'd solve your problem for you and divorce him, leaving Barton free to marry you."

"Sounds rational enough," drawled Mae.

"You drove to Pearl's house, parking the car next door at the park. You were well-familiar with the area, since you were there every afternoon to take Bizzy for a walk. No one would pay any attention to your car with all the others and it was a nice day—it was fairly busy there on a pretty Sunday morning. You walked over to Pearl's house and started talking to her," said Beatrice. "I'm thinking she was aware of Barton's affair because she stayed seated, didn't she?"

Mae languidly nodded. "She was tending to her flowerbed."

"You thought she didn't know about you and Barton and that your announcement that the two of you were in love would shock her. But it wasn't like that, was it?"

"Pearl knew about us. Apparently, Barton had strayed before," said Mae, a hard edge to her voice. "She sounded almost smug when she said that our relationship was merely another affair to Barton and that he always returned to her. That he needed her and that she was essential in his life. That they were a successful partnership and he relied on her."

Beatrice said, "So it was actually *you* who was shocked. You were stunned that Pearl already knew about the affair. You were shocked that Barton had embarked on other affairs because you thought what the two of you shared was special. And you were still reeling from the fact that Barton had ended the relationship. I'm guessing that, on the back end of this surprise, was a lot of fury. You'd been wronged. And it was all because Barton cared for Pearl. He *cheated* on Pearl, yes. But ultimately, he always returned to her because he loved her."

Wyatt had been staring at the two women. He said slowly, "Mae, it sounds as though you never planned on harming Pearl. Was it something completely spontaneous?"

Mae turned her cold eyes on him. "No, it wasn't spontaneous. I'd planned on talking to Pearl ... at first." Her words slurred again and she started speaking again, appearing to make a conscious effort to focus on her speech. "The plan was that I'd reveal that Barton and I were having an affair and also were very much in love." There was scorn in her tone that seemed to be directed at herself. "Wasn't that a brilliant plan? As Beatrice said, I felt that Pearl would be shocked and hurt, perhaps humiliated, and would seek a divorce. Barton would come running back to my arms and we'd live happily ever after." She snorted.

Beatrice said, "But when Plan A didn't work, you moved to Plan B."

"Not *exactly*. Plan B, technically, was to shoot Pearl. I carried a small handgun in my purse. But I realized that the report from the gun would be loud and that we were very close to the park on a busy morning. On the other hand, there was this lovely, large flowerpot nearby. It wouldn't make a sound at all. And, considering the fact that Pearl didn't even think my presence important enough to turn around for, she'd never know what hit her," said Mae.

Ramsay said, "That was a risky approach. You couldn't have been sure that the pot would kill her. And then she'd have told the police about your visit."

Mae raised her eyebrows, eyes droopy. "Oh, I was sure the pot would kill her. I hit her very hard with it because I was very angry. And it was a very large and heavy pot." She settled herself more deeply into her armchair and curled her legs under as if preparing to take a little nap.

Beatrice glanced around the room, taking in the furniture and everything on the tables. She said suddenly, "I'm going to get a glass of water. Is that all right, Mae?"

Mae smiled acidly at her. "Oh please, help yourself. Do make yourself at home."

Bizzy was still barking frantically from the back of the house as if determined to make her presence known and whatever message she was trying desperately to impart.

Beatrice strode into the kitchen and swiftly looked around. She heard Ramsay talking to Mae.

"What happened then?" asked Ramsay. "Did Ophelia come over? I bet she came to apologize, didn't she? Because she had made a scene with Pearl over at my son's wedding. Maybe Ophelia rang the front bell and then walked around the house to the backyard when she heard voices talking. She'd have seen you kill Pearl which would have sealed her own fate."

"I had nothing to do with my Aunt Ophelia's death," said Mae firmly, but still in that oddly slurring voice. "I may not have liked her much, but I didn't kill her."

Beatrice's gaze moved from the kitchen counters to the sink. She opened up the fridge and the pantry. Then she walked out of the kitchen and down a short hall to the bathroom.

Beatrice pushed open the door to the bathroom and turned on the light. There she saw what she was fearfully looking for: four empty bottles of sleeping pills.

Beatrice jogged back to the living room and frantically interrupted Ramsay. "Call 911. Mae has taken a ton of sleeping pills."

Chapter Seventeen

Mae glared furiously at her and jumped up from the armchair, lunging for the door. But the pills had made her sluggish and Beatrice beat her there. Mae struggled against her until Wyatt grabbed her arms and held them firmly as Ramsay put her in handcuffs.

"I'll take her in the cruiser," said Ramsay grimly. "It would take a while for EMS to get here." He turned to Wyatt. "Can you ride with me and help keep her awake while I drive?"

Wyatt nodded, handing Beatrice the car keys as Ramsay hustled Mae into the back of the police car.

"Take care of Bizzy," said Mae in a surprisingly clear voice. "Beatrice? Do you hear me?"

"I do," said Beatrice. Although she wasn't entirely sure what taking care of Bizzy entailed.

Mae seemed to realize this. "Find her a good home. The best. I won't be coming home again," she said as Ramsay shut the door.

Mae peered entreatingly through the window and Beatrice nodded at her as the car took off at high speed.

Beatrice walked back into Mae's house and toward the barking, which sounded pitifully insistent now. She opened the bedroom door and saw the little Pekingese staring up at her.

"Here, it's all right," said Beatrice, gently picking up the tiny dog. "Let's pack your bags. It's going to be all right. You'll like visiting with Noo-noo. And then we'll find someone who will love you and take care of you."

For the next few minutes, Beatrice found Bizzy's bed, crate, bowls, harness and leash, brush, toys, and food. The little dog settled down, but was still shivering.

Beatrice carefully set Bizzy's crate in the passenger side of the front seat so that Bizzy could watch her as she drove home. But before she'd even turned on the engine, she had a text from Wyatt.

"Think Mae is doing all right. Received word from the woman who runs the exercise class that she's sick tonight and class is canceled. Could you run by Violet's and let her know not to head out for the church nursery? She's not answering her texts and I can't call right now in present circumstances."

No, Wyatt was in no position to call anyone. Beatrice started her engine and her phone rang simultaneously. Meadow's name popped up on her phone. Beatrice sighed, but picked up. "Meadow? I can't talk right now—I'm about to start driving."

"Is something going on?" demanded Meadow. "Ramsay was supposed to be home long before now."

"He's fine. I ran into him while I was out. Listen, I'll give you a call back as soon as I get back home. I need to run an errand to Violet's house for Wyatt really quickly." Beatrice hung up in the middle of Meadow's spluttering.

Beatrice pulled into the driveway of Violet's modest house. She saw that her car was in the driveway and glanced at her watch. Violet would likely be setting off for the church any minute, considering when the exercise class usually started. "Bizzy? I'll be right back." Not a fan of leaving dogs in cars, she carefully took the crate and set it outside the car. She walked up the short walkway to Violet's front door.

She raised her hand to knock, but paused at the sound of arguing inside. Beatrice leaned closer to the door. She could hear two voices inside and Violet's voice sounded frantic. Beatrice could hear her crying inside. She couldn't place the other voice, though. Bizzy gave a low growl, but didn't bark.

Beatrice looked back at the driveway and street. There was no car besides Violet's so someone must have taken trouble to conceal him or herself. Beatrice hesitated. She felt as though she should slip inside and assess the situation without either of them seeing her, but she didn't want to go inside without some sort of weapon. Her mind combed over everything that was in her car. There was nothing in there aside from her purse and a couple of books in the backseat. And Bizzy's belongings were hardly going to help.

Beatrice walked around to the front of the house again, remembering that Violet's garage had been open. She glanced around inside. There were brooms and mops, but those weren't going to be good enough. Her gaze stopped on the ax, but she shuddered. Maybe as a last resort. Then she saw a post hole digger and grabbed it. It was heavy enough to knock someone out if she swung it at them.

Instead of heading back to the front door, Beatrice tried the garage door and found it unlocked. She cautiously opened it since she didn't know where the door led to, although she didn't hear the voices as loudly as she had at the front of the house. Sure enough, it opened into the kitchen and the voices were coming from the living room.

Beatrice held the digger in front of her and walked closer to the voices. She could hear Bizzy's small barks, but the people inside seemed too focused on their argument to notice.

"You can't do this," pleaded Violet's tearful voice. "They'll find out that it was you. I'm supposed to be at the church in a few minutes to watch the nursery. They'll see what you've done and they'll find you."

Beatrice waited to listen for the other voice, hoping to identify the owner of it. But she had a sickening feeling that she knew who it was. She'd thought about Violet's surprise again during an earlier conversation and how incongruous that had been. And then a sharp look of concern when she'd mentioned Violet's surprise.

She listened for the voice she knew was coming. And felt saddened when she heard Lois say in a rough voice, "There's nothing I can do. You know that. And I can't have you knowing. Besides, I didn't even park nearby ... I walked. No one knows that I'm here."

Chapter Eighteen

"**I** won't say a word, Lois! I won't tell anyone. I didn't even know that you were connected to Ophelia's death ... I wasn't sure why you told everyone that you'd been pushed down the stairs when I knew that you'd fallen. I figured that maybe you just wanted to get some attention or something." Violet's laugh was more like a sob. "Just let me go. I'm just now figuring my life out and trying to be a better person. Don't cut that short."

Lois snapped at her, "Do you think it's easy for me? I didn't want any of this to happen. I'm just as much a victim as you are."

Violet continued, her voice shaky, "You aren't a killer, Lois. You've just been pushed into it. Tell you what. I'll tell you my deepest, darkest secret since I know yours. Believe me, I don't want it out any more than you want *yours* out. Then we'll know we'll both stay quiet."

Lois said in a flat voice, "I really don't think that's going to work."

"It's a pretty big secret," said Violet desperately. "I burned down Mona's shed. I was furious with her and I burned it down."

Lois said briskly, "That's pretty horrible, but not exactly in the same league as murder."

Beatrice carefully peered around the door into the living room with her finger over her mouth to warn Violet if she spotted her. She saw Lois's back to her. Lois held what looked like a poker from Violet's fireplace and she wore gloves.

Violet's tear-filled eyes flew to Beatrice's face and she made a startled cry of recognition.

Lois spun around and that's when Beatrice lunged forward, swinging the post hole digger with all her might at the poker that Lois held. It clattered on the floor and Beatrice kicked it away, still brandishing the digger at Lois.

Violet gave a shuddering cry and stumbled away from Lois and behind Beatrice. "She's lost it," she panted. "She was going to kill me. You saw, didn't you?"

Beatrice nodded, eyes still trained on Lois. "I did, unfortunately. Lois, I can hardly believe it of you. You were always such a good friend to Piper and have always seemed like you had your head screwed on right."

Lois's eyes narrowed and she gazed furiously back at Beatrice. "I guess everyone has their breaking point. Even Violet here burned down a shed."

Violet gave a little embarrassed moan and said, "Beatrice, I'm planning on making up for that. I'm going to confess to Mona and pay her restitution. I've been trying to do better. I'm turning over a new leaf. We talked about that."

Beatrice continued watching Lois. Her voice was calm as she said to Violet, "I know you'll put things right. Can you place a phone call for me to the police? Ramsay is in his car now, but the deputy should be available."

While Violet stepped back into the kitchen to talk to the police, Beatrice asked Lois, "So what was *your* breaking point? You said that everyone has one."

"I suppose that Ophelia was my breaking point," said Lois. "Obviously."

Beatrice said, "You'd already mentioned that you weren't happy teaching. You'd enjoyed working for Barton before and this time he offered to take you on again if he were to win the election. But something stood in your way ... or, rather, some*one*. Ophelia was the nosiest person in Dappled Hills. She made it her business to get in everyone else's business. If she spread damaging gossip about you, you weren't even going to be able to get a job *teaching*, much less a position for Barton. I'm thinking that must have been something illegal, not immoral. It wouldn't have been an affair. Maybe it was theft? Drugs?"

Violet came back into the living room and hovered by the kitchen door as if ready to escape at any moment.

Lois said harshly, "You really *are* a Miss Marple, aren't you? But you're very right. It wasn't an affair. The school would hardly fire me for such an offense and Barton couldn't exactly blame me for having an affair if he was having one himself ... if the gossip is all true. Apparently, I'm a much weaker person than you and Piper think, Beatrice. It was drugs. I'd been involved with drugs when I was a teenager and fell in with the wrong crowd." She gave a derisive snort. "Or maybe *I* was the wrong crowd. Anyway, it made it that much easier to fall off the wagon when it seemed as though everything was going wrong with my life."

Beatrice said, "You'd just had a failed relationship with someone that you cared about. You weren't happy teaching, which you'd formerly considered your dream job. Nothing seemed as though it was going right for you. You slipped back into your old habits. Although I can't imagine that Dappled Hills has a drug dealer in it. You must have driven somewhere out of town."

"Lenoir," said Lois. "Of course, the idea was that I would also be avoiding the prying eyes of people in Dappled Hills. Instead, the person with the most prying of all the eyes was there to see me."

"Ophelia," said Violet, shaking her head.

"That's right. She should have just minded her own business. She was in Lenoir for some sort of medical treatment—an MRI or something. I guess she got lost since I can't think of a single reason she'd have been in the section of town that I was in. Anyway, she saw me getting drugs and even managed to take a picture," said Lois in disgust.

Beatrice said, "Did Ophelia immediately confront you about it?"

"Oh no. No, she was like a cat with a mouse, just toying with me over it. The first time that I saw her in town she gave me this mysterious smile and said something about 'hidden depths.' I thought she was simply going a little senile, so I left it alone. I hadn't seen her in Lenoir, so I had no idea what she was talking about."

"But then she started getting more specific," said Beatrice.

"Right. She came up to me when I was leaving the school and said that it was such a shame that a teacher would have such terrible morals, or something like that. I demanded to know what she was talking about and she showed me the picture that she'd taken of me in Lenoir," said Lois.

Beatrice said, "Ophelia didn't want to blackmail you, though."

"No. As she said at Piper's wedding, she didn't need the money. She simply liked torturing people with information that she'd discovered. And she'd really found a gold mine when she saw me taking part in a drug deal," said Lois darkly.

"What do you think her end goal was?" asked Beatrice.

"To ruin my life," said Lois simply. "She definitely wanted to manipulate me behind the scenes. Ophelia wanted me to quit my job ... she didn't realize that I'd wanted to quit it anyway. And she wanted to make sure that I knew she could reveal more and more little sordid details about my visit to Lenoir whenever she wanted and to whomever she wished."

Beatrice said, "So you paid her a visit. Perhaps you thought that Pearl would even be a suspect, considering her public altercation with Ophelia at the wedding."

"Why not?" said Lois with a shrug.

"Ophelia invited you inside. I'm imagining her being somewhat lighthearted and relaxed," said Beatrice. She could hear the sound of sirens in the distance.

Lois said derisively, "Of course she was. That's because she thought she had me in the palm of her hand. She was Miss High and Mighty."

"And she was so relaxed that she made the mistake of turning her back on you. If Ophelia had any idea what you'd planned, she never would have taken her eyes off of you," said Beatrice.

"If she'd had any idea what I'd planned, she never would have opened the door," said Lois. "Silly woman. If I had any doubts about what I was doing, those went right out of my head as soon as I arrived at her house and started talking with her. Ophelia was so hateful about the drugs. And she was so holier than thou."

Beatrice said, "And you saw a large bottle of wine in her kitchen."

"Exactly! What a hypocrite. She led everyone to believe that she never touched a drop of alcohol, when clearly she was drinking as much as she wanted," said Lois.

Violet ventured from the kitchen, "That's what killed her, wasn't it? The wine bottle?"

Beatrice said, "It made the perfect weapon. Lois was hoping on finding something at Ophelia's house that would work as a weapon. That's what she did here, Violet, with the poker. That way she's not drawing any attention to herself walking in and there's nothing really to get rid of afterward. Ophelia turned her back on Lois to go down her hall and that's when Lois struck. Then Lois turned the house upside-down to try and find any notes or pictures of herself. Anything that might give away her motive for the murder."

Lois said, "Not that Ophelia was the best record-keeper. I couldn't find anything but the photo."

"But you did find Ophelia's stash of money. You decided to take that money and hide it away so that it would look as if robbery were the motive. The house was already trashed and it was obvious that the killer was looking for something. By taking that money, you were able to create a distraction," said Beatrice.

Violet asked, "Where did that money go? Do you still have it, Lois?"

Beatrice said, "Lois actually ditched it in the woods off a trail. Wyatt and I stumbled into it while we were out walking my dog."

Lois snorted. "Of course you did."

Beatrice said, "You could probably have kept the money. It wasn't as if it could have been traced."

Lois said, "But it wasn't *about* the money. And I didn't need money bad enough to have wanted to profit from a crime."

Beatrice continued, "You had other things on your mind besides the money, didn't you. You worried that you were becoming too much of a suspect. There was evidence leading to you, after all—Ophelia did jot down a few notes about Dappled Hills residents, even though you didn't come across them. She kept the notes as a bookmark. Ophelia also negatively compared you with another suspect in a public place. Still, it didn't seem as though you had much motive. You couldn't resist trying to throw suspicion off of you, though, and decided to fake an accident. That's when you started getting into trouble."

Violet nodded. "I saw that fall from a distance. I wasn't close by, but I was close enough to see that no one had pushed Lois. I didn't realize that she was going around telling people that she'd been pushed until I ran into you, Beatrice."

"And, unfortunately, I told Lois that you'd been surprised about being shoved. Lois realized that you must have seen that it was an accidental fall. She couldn't allow you to say anything to the police, so she came here tonight," said Beatrice.

"Well done," said Lois in a sarcastic voice. "You really are a Nancy Drew, aren't you?"

A car door slammed outside and the sound of footsteps approached.

Violet said, "And I never would have been able to say what I'd seen. Beatrice, you saved my life. What made you decide to come here tonight?"

Beatrice gave a short laugh. "Wyatt couldn't reach you on the phone and knew I was out. He wanted to make sure you didn't go to the church to watch the nursery ... the exercise class is cancelled." For once, she was glad that the church didn't have its admin assistant yet.

Chapter Nineteen

Ramsay's deputy came in, took one look at the scene in front of him with Beatrice brandishing the post hole digger at Lois, and quickly pulled out his handcuffs and slid them on Lois.

"What makes me the saddest," said Beatrice, "is having to explain all of this to Piper when she comes back from her honeymoon."

Lois couldn't seem to muster a reply, her earlier bravado disappearing in the face of her arrest.

The deputy took Lois away and then Ramsay returned from Lenoir with Wyatt to take Violet's statement first, and then Beatrice's statement while Violet rested inside and Wyatt went inside to talk with her for a few minutes, as her minister.

Beatrice held Bizzy in her arms as she sat on Violet's front porch and recounted her story. She had to admit that petting the long-haired Pekingese was very de-stressing.

Ramsay shook his head after she finished. He put the cap back on his pen. "This has been quite a day. Two different murders with two different murderers. That's pretty extraordinary. I was still thinking it could still be the same one."

Beatrice said, "It's not quite as much of a coincidence as it seems. The thing that tied them together was Ophelia's argument with Pearl. That was witnessed by Lois and heard about in town by Mae. Both of them used it as an opportunity to deflect any suspicion from themselves and onto Pearl or Ophelia. But it didn't work out that way."

Ramsay said, "They must have been upset when they found out the 'suspect' they were trying to set up was dead."

"I'm sure it must have been a bad moment for both of them. But they both had secrets and were pretty good at keeping them hidden. I guess they thought that they'd be able to continue concealing them. Mae hoped that no one knew about the affair and that she could convince Barton to come back to her. Lois hoped that no one but Ophelia knew about her drug habit and that she could get a job with Barton after he won his election," said Beatrice.

Ramsay said, "Unfortunately, with Mae's arrest, it might be hard for Barton to overcome any scandal, at least here in Dappled Hills."

"That's true. In a town this size, everyone tomorrow morning will be aware that Mae was arrested for Pearl's murder. That's going to start tongues wagging, for sure," said Beatrice.

Ramsay said, "And I guess I'll notify the school that Lois won't be teaching there tomorrow ... or at any point. They're going to need to find a substitute and then another permanent teacher. And you said that Lois told you that she had a prior drug habit?" Ramsay glanced down at his notebook, full of scribbles.

"Exactly. Apparently, she'd had some substance issues during her teen years, and again when she'd gotten so stressed out about school, her failed relationship, and the direction her life was taking, she fell back into the habit," said Beatrice.

Ramsay said, "I wonder if Ophelia's death could have been prevented. It sounded as if Mae was planning on ending Pearl's life, regardless, but I keep thinking that Ophelia's murder was different."

"If Ophelia had been reasonable, maybe. If she'd assured Lois that her life was her business and instead encouraged Lois to get some help, maybe things would have worked out differently. Instead, from everything I understand, Ophelia was taunting Lois over it. She wanted to have control over Lois's life. She tried to manipulate her into quitting her teaching job before Lois had another job lined up. Lois found an opportunity when Ophelia had turned her back on her and took advantage of it," said Beatrice.

Ramsay said, "And later faked her accident just to keep suspicion off of her." He gave a disgusted snort.

"I think she was worried. We'd also found all the stuff that she'd stolen to keep us thinking that it was a financially-motived crime when it wasn't. She wanted to make sure that her future plans weren't going to be thwarted," said Beatrice.

"Well, they sure are now, for a long time. And Mae's, too. It's a shame," said Ramsay with a shake of his head. He glanced at his watch. "I have the feeling that you two are probably ready to head on home now. You were here at the beginning of these cases and now you're here for the close of them."

Wyatt came outside to join them.

Ramsay looked at Bizzy. "What are you going to do about the Bizzy situation?"

"I'm bringing her home with Wyatt and me, for tonight anyway. Then I've got to figure out who would provide a good home."

Wyatt said slowly, "You know, Violet was just saying that she was uncomfortable being alone in the house tonight. And she's mentioned feeling lonely to me, too. I wonder if she likes dogs at all."

"She was certainly crazy about Noo-noo when she saw her. Do you think it's too much though, after all she's been through tonight? Bizzy might end up crying all night for Mae. Violet might not get any sleep," said Beatrice.

Wyatt said, "I have the feeling that Violet isn't going to be doing a whole lot of sleeping, anyway."

"I'll go ask her," said Beatrice, picking up Bizzy and carrying her into Violet's house.

Violet was sitting quietly in an armchair and had turned on the gas fireplace as if the stress had made her chilly. She had poured herself a small glass of white wine. When she caught sight of Bizzy, she stood up. "What a beautiful dog! I didn't know that you had two dogs, Beatrice."

Beatrice gently handed the Pekingese over to Violet and watched as Violet laid her head on her soft fur. "Actually, I *don't* have two dogs ... just Noo-noo. But Mae asked me to find a home for her Bizzy."

Violet's face turned serious. "Ramsay filled me in on what happened with Mae. What a mess." She hesitated and looked shyly at Beatrice. "I don't even feel right asking this, but would you consider letting me have Bizzy? Or at least seeing if the arrangement works out well for both Bizzy and me? I know you must be thinking terrible things about me after what Lois told you about the shed. It's just that I'm so alone here in this house. I'm trying to rebuild my friendships, but it's going to take some time. If I could just have someone to talk to when I come back home, it would be so much better. I know I work a lot, but I come and go from the house all day long and will have plenty of time to take Bizzy out and exercise her."

Beatrice was about to bring up the fact that Bizzy might bark or cry all night for Mae when she saw the little dog reach up and nuzzle Violet's neck. Violet's eyes filled with tears.

Beatrice said gruffly before her own eyes filled up, "I've only seen you be very tender with animals, Violet. Of course you can have Bizzy for a trial run. Let me or Wyatt know how it works out for the two of you."

Violet reached out and gave Beatrice a hug, giving a wordless cry.

Beatrice said, "I'll bring in all of Bizzy's paraphernalia. She has quite a bit." But Violet was too absorbed in the little dog to even hear her.

A few minutes later, Wyatt brought in Bizzy's things and made sure Violet had their phone number in case she needed anything.

Ramsay watched as Wyatt and Beatrice got into Beatrice's car. "Now, if you *want* to, you can always fill Meadow in, Beatrice. That'll save me the hassle. Only if you're up to it, though. You've had a long day."

Beatrice smiled at him as she started the car. "I think I will call her. Better than having her come over to visit us at seven in the morning, right?"

She backed out of Violet's driveway and headed back home. Wyatt quietly reached out and put his hand on her leg.

"You don't know how relieved I am that everything went okay at Violet's house. To think that I could have lost you." He broke off and shook his head.

Beatrice said, "Believe me, I'm glad that everything went okay, too. There was a moment or two there when I thought it might not have had such a happy ending. I think I was just so focused on trying to make sure Violet wasn't going to be murdered right in front of my eyes that I didn't put as much stock into my own safety. But I was so glad when I ended up with the upper hand and had Violet there to back me up and the police on the way."

Wyatt gently squeezed her arm and they rode through the night in silence for a minute.

Then Beatrice said with a grin, "How about this for a radical idea? Instead of finding victims and stopping murderers this week, I'll finish quilting Piper and Ash's Christmas presents and you'll preach a sermon and minister to the congregation?"

Wyatt smiled back at her. "It sounds like the best week ever."

About the Author:

Elizabeth writes the Southern Quilting mysteries and Memphis Barbeque mysteries for Penguin Random House and the Myrtle Clover series for Midnight Ink and independently. She blogs at ElizabethSpannCraig.com/blog, named by Writer's Digest as one of the 101 Best Websites for Writers. Elizabeth makes her home in Matthews, North Carolina, with her husband. She's the mother of two.

Sign up for Elizabeth's free newsletter to stay updated on releases:

https://elizabethspanncraig.com/newsletter/

This and That

I love hearing from my readers. You can find me on Facebook as Elizabeth Spann Craig Author, on Twitter as elizabethscraig, on my website at elizabethspanncraig.com, and by email at elizabethspanncraig@gmail.com.

Thanks so much for reading my book...I appreciate it. If you enjoyed the story, would you please leave a short review on the site where you purchased it? Just a few words would be great. Not only do I feel encouraged reading them, but they also help other readers discover my books. Thank you!

Did you know my books are available in print and ebook formats? And most of the Myrtle Clover series is available in audio. Find them on Audible or iTunes.

Interested in having a character named after you? In a preview of my books before they're released? Or even just your name listed in the acknowledgments of a future book? Visit my Patreon page at https://www.patreon.com/elizabethspanncraig .

I have Myrtle Clover tote bags, charms, magnets, and other goodies at my Café Press shop: https://www.cafepress.com/cozymystery

If you'd like an autographed book for yourself or a friend, please visit my Etsy page.

I'd also like to thank some folks who helped me put this book together. Thanks to my cover designer, Karri Klawiter, for her awesome covers. Thanks to my editor, Judy Beatty, for all of her help. Thanks to beta readers Amanda Arrieta and Dan Harris for all of their helpful suggestions and careful reading. Thanks, as always, to my family and readers.

Other Works by the Author:

Myrtle Clover Series in Order (be sure to look for the Myrtle series in audio, ebook, and print):

Pretty is as Pretty Dies

Progressive Dinner Deadly

A Dyeing Shame

A Body in the Backyard

Death at a Drop-In

A Body at Book Club

Death Pays a Visit

A Body at Bunco

Murder on Opening Night

Cruising for Murder

Cooking is Murder

A Body in the Trunk

Cleaning is Murder

Edit to Death

Southern Quilting Mysteries in Order:

Quilt or Innocence

Knot What it Seams

Quilt Trip

Shear Trouble

Tying the Knot

Patch of Trouble

Fall to Pieces

Rest in Pieces

On Pins and Needles

Fit to be Tied

The Village Library Mysteries in Order (Debuting 2019):

Checked Out (2019)

Memphis Barbeque Mysteries in Order (Written as Riley Adams):

Delicious and Suspicious

Finger Lickin' Dead

Hickory Smoked Homicide

Rubbed Out

And a standalone "cozy zombie" novel: Race to Refuge, written as Liz Craig

Made in the USA
Monee, IL
05 June 2022